Donald MacKenzie and The Murder Room

>>> This title is part of The Murder Room, our series dedicated to making available out-of-print or hard-to-find titles by classic crime writers.

Crime fiction has always held up a mirror to society. The Victorians were fascinated by sensational murder and the emerging science of detection; now we are obsessed with the forensic detail of violent death. And no other genre has so captivated and enthralled readers.

Vast troves of classic crime writing have for a long time been unavailable to all but the most dedicated frequenters of second-hand bookshops. The advent of digital publishing means that we are now able to bring you the backlists of a huge range of titles by classic and contemporary crime writers, some of which have been out of print for decades.

From the genteel amateur private eyes of the Golden Age and the femmes fatales of pulp fiction, to the morally ambiguous hard-boiled detectives of mid twentieth-century America and their descendants who walk our twenty-first century streets, The Murder Room has it all. **>>>**

The Murder Room
Where Criminal Minds Meet

themurderroom.com

T0345492

Donald MacKenzie 1908–1994

Donald MacKenzie was born in Ontario, Canada, and educated in England, Canada and Switzerland. For twenty-five years MacKenzie lived by crime in many countries. 'I went to jail,' he wrote, 'if not with depressing regularity, too often for my liking.' His last sentences were five years in the United States and three years in England, running consecutively. He began writing and selling stories when in American jail. 'I try to do exactly as I like as often as possible and I don't think I'm either psychopathic, a wayward boy, a problem of our time, a charming rogue. Or ever was.'

He had a wife, Estrela, and a daughter, and they divided their time between England, Portugal, Spain and Austria.

Raven Settles a Score

Donald MacKenzie

An Orion book

Copyright © The Estate of Donald MacKenzie 1979

The right of Donald MacKenzie to be identified as the author of this work has been asserted in accordance with the Copyright, Designs and Patents Act 1988.

This edition published by
The Orion Publishing Group Ltd
Orion House
5 Upper St Martin's Lane
London WC2H 9EA

An Hachette UK company
A CIP catalogue record for this book is available from the British Library

ISBN 978 1 4719 0507 0

www.orionbooks.co.uk

JOHN RAVEN

July 18

It was ten o'clock at night with the *Albatross* gently bumping the old truck tyres that protected her hull from the granite blocks of the Embankment. Strings of lights spanned the river in both directions. The converted barge had once been used to haul beer, and the heat of the day released a faint vinegary tang from the timbers. Raven and Soo had finished their meal and were sitting out on deck. Both men were naked except for their swimming trunks. Their bodies were brown. Soo's because this was the colour of his skin, Raven's from the sun. He had put on weight over the last few months, most of it in the wrong places. And the grey streaks in his long toffee-coloured hair had increased and whitened.

He pushed his deck-chair back, looking up at the sky. The moon was in its First Quarter and the stars were brighter than usual. There were more flowers on deck this summer. Raven had grown them in anything that would hold earth. The sweet and mellow perfume came from a mass of stocks he had planted in an old bassinet.

'There's something about a night like this,' he said, looking down at the Chinaman lying beside him. 'It's something the bastards can never take away from us. How long have we known one another, Jerry?'

Jerry Soo rolled over, a wide-shouldered man with bandy legs. 'Seventeen years, man and boy.'

Raven nodded to himself, looking back at the

stars. 'We talk. We don't talk. Friendship's a funny thing when you think about it.'

Soo belched loudly into the night. He rapped himself on the chest.

'That food's given me heartburn. That comes of buying King's Road Chinese takeaway cooked by a Moroccan chef.'

The mudflats across the river sent a whiff of the sea. They had swum together before eating, splashing like boys in the dark ebbing water. Raven's trunks were still damp.

'You know the one thing you've got that I haven't?' he asked suddenly.

Soo gave it some thought. 'The one thing I've got that you haven't? You're talking about problems, obviously.'

The smell of hash on the wind was stronger than the scent of the flowers. The owner of the neighbouring boat was a gentle Californian who owned the Herborium on the north side of the Embankment. He dyed his beard green, meditated and lived with a daft Great Dane he called Bogdan.

'What kind of problems could you conceivably have?' demanded Raven. 'You've got a beautiful woman in love with you, your own teeth and you're getting paid under false pretences, doing a job that you like. How do you get a problem out of that?'

They had been at Hendon Police College together, selected for the ten-week course at the Detective Training School. Each had been a misfit in his own way, Raven because of his upper-class background, the Hong Kong-born recruit because of his race and foreign upbringing. They had grown close and protected one another over the years. Raven's friendship with Soo was the only thing he had taken with him when he resigned from the Force. It was a comradeship that he shared with nobody else. You asked from need and were given. It was as simple as that.

'I suppose the real difference is that you're doing what you want,' said Raven, slapping the mosquitoes away from his neck.

Soo was lying flat on his back, stomach-muscles bulging as he lifted his legs with the toes pointing. He exhaled noisily.

'You're still singing the same old song, I hear. The gentleman policeman yearning for his pair of handcuffs.'

Raven placed a foot on the other man's legs, forcing them down.

'Don't give me the "gentleman cop" routine. You sound like Drake. For your information, my grandfather sold corn by the bushel. The nearest he got to being a gentleman was an iron statue in front of the local drill-hall. I repeat. You are doing a job that you like and getting paid for it. I'm not envious of the job particularly. I'm envious of the chase.'

The four rooms, kitchen and bath had been built into a cedarwood superstructure. The double-glazed sitting room was forty feet long with two doors that opened on to the deck, one on each side. The one on the port side was open. The sound of the record-player drifted out. Soo crossed his ankles and rose to his feet without using his hands.

'That's the fifth time tonight you've played *Les Franc Juges* and I say the hell with Berlioz!'

He padded into the sitting room and removed the arm of the record-player. His voice was suddenly gentle.

'What's the matter with you, John? It isn't Cathy again, is it?'

Raven shook his head. 'It is *not* Cathy. Miss Leeds is dead and gone.' He could say it without a tremor, her ghost finally laid. Her things had been cleared from the guest room and the feeling of guilt had vanished.

'Then what?' Soo resumed his place on the deck, hands locked behind his head.

Raven shifted a shoulder. 'You could call it a general feeling of *malaise*, I suppose.'

'A general feeling of *malaise*,' Soo repeated sarcastically. 'What a lot of bollocks you sometimes talk, John! You know damn well that you couldn't have stayed on the Force after that Zaleski business. Drake was always going to have your guts for garters.'

Raven blew a stream of cigarette smoke at the stars. He could talk about Cathy now without feeling, but Drake's name still made the adrenalin rush.

'I suppose that bastard's still around, poisoning the atmosphere?'

'Very much so,' said Soo. 'The Commander sits on Promotion Boards, drinks with Assistant Commissioners, and there's a strong rumour afoot that he's going on to even higher things.'

Raven grunted. He followed the spiralling red tip of his cigarette as it disappeared over the side.

'Do you know what a Promotion Board once said about me, Jerry? They said I was a born enforcer of law and order. Which shows how little they knew.

4

I'm a hunter not an enforcer. I suppose if I'd wanted to play their miserable game I could still be at the Yard.'

Soo's hand wagged dissent. 'Never in a million years. You broke too many rules, gave too many people the raspberry.'

'And you?' The shaft of light from the sitting room shone on the Chinaman's face. The absence of lids showing gave his eyes the fixed look of a hawk.

'I only bend rules,' said Soo. 'You made a production of breaking them. That's the reason I'm in and you're out. Come to think of it, you're not doing too badly,' he added.

The noise of the traffic was loud now that the music had stopped. The weight of the heavy trucks shook the foundations of the riverside houses.

'How's Louise?' asked Raven.

Soo's girlfriend was a Taiwanese of frail beauty who played cello in the London Philharmonic Orchestra.

'She's all right,' said Soo. 'In fact she's getting married. Some time next year, I hear.'

Raven jerked up straight. 'Getting married to *who*?'

'Me,' Soo said complacently.

The news was strangely disturbing. It wasn't that Raven didn't like Louise. She had been living with Jerry for more than two years and had never been a threat to their friendship. She encouraged them to continue taking their vacations together. Hong Kong this year, the Dolomites next. But marriage was something else, a barrier that would keep him out.

'Congratulations,' he said and hoped it sounded sincere.

'Come to think of it,' there was a grin in Soo's voice, 'you should be the one to marry her. She could play her cello for you and you could go to all those concerts together. And you both drink whisky.'

He collected Raven's glass, refilled it from the decanter in the sitting room and poured himself another Pernod.

'This'll be my last. I'd better be moving.'

The surface of the river reflected the lights of the neighbouring houseboats.

'I don't know, Jerry,' Raven said suddenly.

'You're bored again,' said Soo. 'That's all that's the matter with you.'

Raven made a long-arm, reaching for his cigarettes. There was only one left in the pack. He was trying to cut down on his smoking and drinking, and jogging a mile every morning.

'I'm in a rut, Jerry,' he said. 'I'm doing the same bloody things every day. Even going out with the same ladies. I'm not forty yet but I'm running out of ideas. I'm starting to conform, my friend. The great nonconformer's starting to conform.'

Soo held his glass up to the light, swirled the ice in the cloudy liquid.

'You really think you're hard done by, don't you? You eat what you like, go to bed when you like, get up when you like. You can walk into a pub without running the risk of some hoodlum stepping up behind you and removing your head with a razor. Take tonight, for instance. You don't want to be

6

disturbed so what do you do, take the phone off the hook and leave it there. *I* can't do that.'

It was true. Police regulations required a cop to be on call twenty-four hours a day. Raven sighed. The breeze was warm on his bare skin. It was hard to explain even to Jerry.

'There's more to life than going to bed and getting up, taking the bloody phone off the hook. It's the hunt that I miss, Jerry. I was thinking about putting an advertisement in the newspaper. "Ex-C.I.D. Inspector" – I don't even know what comes next.'

Soo yawned. 'Ex-C.I.D. Inspector gives lessons in self-pity?'

Raven shook his head. 'You're too insensitive to understand.'

Soo came up on his elbows. 'We don't get too much of the hunt in C 11. In fact if a real live thief walked into the office I'd probably ask for his autograph. I'm off. It's past eleven and Louise will be waiting.'

'She'll learn,' said Raven.

Soo vanished into the guest room. He reappeared dressed in tight jeans and a T-shirt bearing the inscription THE YELLOW PERIL. Somehow he managed to make the outfit appear respectable. Raven saw him to the end of the gangway. Soo's beefed-up mini was parked on the opposite side of the Embankment. They shook hands as they always did, Raven craning down to Soo's modest height.

'Take care,' said Raven. 'And drive carefully.'

'I always do,' grinned Soo. 'And thanks for the Moroccan chop suey.'

RODERIC CAMPBELL

July 19

He left his small black Fiat at the north end of the square. The last of the sun was shining through the tall iron railings that enclosed the tree-shaded gardens and tennis court. The gates in the railings were locked, the gardens accessible only to those tenants who had been issued with keys. It was ten minutes past six by the watch on Campbell's right wrist. He had another twenty minutes to wait. The traffic wardens had gone off duty.

He loped across to the nearest gate, a six-footer in his early thirties with ginger hair and marmalade freckles. He was wearing a pair of clean, mended jeans, sneakers and sweatshirt and carried a tennis racket under his left arm. He opened the gate with a key. Like the other three on the ring, he had made it from the cuttle-bone impressions Arbela had taken for him.

Two teenage girls were on the tennis court, batting balls across the net at one another. He took a seat on a bench under a lilac tree, well away from the black-shrouded Arab hag with eye-and-nose shield who crouched near a pram. Beyond the railings facing him was a five-storey house constructed of red brick and with a basement area. The windows on the lower floors were heavily curtained. A striped awning protected the door at the top of the entrance steps.

He raised his head a little, squinting through the acrid cloud of cigarette smoke. The chancellery of the North Korean Embassy occupied the lower floors while the Ambassador and his wife, together with two servants lived in the top part of the house. Campbell glanced down at his hands, aware of the increasing pressure driving the blood through his veins. His fingers were steady enough. He had burgled the house across the street twice in as many days, though 'burgled' was maybe the wrong word to use. 'Fitted it up' was better. All he had done was try the keys he had made, disturbing nothing, stealing not so much as a dime. He had stood in the dim hallway, unseen and unsuspected, the faint light from the transom revealing the fat curves of the carved-wood Buddha. Hanging on the wall behind were photographs of sinister-looking men with slit eyes set in square faces. A distinctive odour permeated the hallway and he traced it to the elevator. The blended whiff of dried fish and ginger-root was reminiscent of his native Vancouver.

On neither occasion had he gone any further than the door sealing the foot of the staircase that led to the second storey. His keys had worked perfectly. Arbela had drawn a detailed plan of the secretariat. Her office was next to the Ambassador's private room and the safe. The small French-type elevator served all floors up to the residential quarters. The gates opened on to doors that were always kept locked. He already knew the make of the safe and its size. What he needed now was the kind of information Arbela could never supply. She lacked the expertise involved. Only close inspection would tell him how best to open fifteen tons of time-locked heat-resistant steel. Hidden under a rose bush in the garden of his mews house was a canister containing four kilos of *Peralite* and a package of Czech detonators.

Explosives were new to him. He'd never used them in his life. It had taken the French to show him how, demonstrating in a rain-soaked quarry near Nantes. They had even stolen an empty safe for the purpose. The demonstration had been spectacular, with little noise and practically no flash. The safe had simply buckled at the seams and joints. *Peralite* was plastic-based and developed for the French armed forces. Its sale on the open market was strictly prohibited. Campbell borrowed a thousand pounds to pay for it, putting up his house as collateral. It seemed little enough when he made his calculations. It had been hard to believe the sort of money Arbela had said that she'd seen in the safe, the sum that she'd checked on the adding machine. But she wasn't a liar. In fact her information had come as a sort of aside, an off-the-cuff remark that had straightened him in his chair. The moment she realized his interest in what she had said she wanted to forget the whole thing. But he'd gone at her like a terrier, backing her into a corner and shaking the truth from her till at last he realized exactly what she was saying. She was telling him that here was the final score every thief dreams about, the last payoff that will take him away across town.

He checked his watch again. Six-thirty. He came to his feet, moving to the right of the lilac tree, still hidden but able to observe the Mercedes limousine that had drawn up in front of the embassy entrance.

The chauffeur opened the rear door for an Oriental couple dressed in Western clothing. Campbell knew the man and woman by sight as the Ambassador and his wife. The limousine drove off. Campbell watched it out of the square and felt in his hip-pocket. The contours of the keyring reassured him. The embassy office staff went home at five o'clock, the cleaners at six. He had been watching the house for a week now. During that time, the Ambassador and his wife had gone out on no less than five evenings.

Campbell had tailed the official car on each occasion, twice to a Korean restaurant deep in the East End, once to a theatre, a couple of times to embassy parties. The Ambassador's absence left four people in the embassy. The servants upstairs, and the two security guards who lived and slept in the basement. At nine o'clock precisely one of the guards started his rounds of the building and the garden behind. He repeated the performance at three-hourly intervals. The rest of the time, he sat on a chair in the hallway, completing his tour of duty at eight o'clock the following morning.

Between the hours of six and nine at night, the security measures protecting the embassy were practically non-existent. Campbell's plan was to hit the safe while the Ambassador and his wife were out. He figured that the point of danger started at the moment of explosion and reached its peak as he made his getaway. He calculated that it should take him no more than two minutes to clear the safe. The security guard on duty would be in a quandary. If he chose to stay below when he heard the explosion, either in the basement or the hallway, Campbell would drop from a second-storey window, landing on the roof of the squash courts next door. A ten-second dash from there would take him to safety. On the other hand, if the guard used the elevator Campbell took the stairs down and vice versa.

He unlocked the gate in the railings, doing his best to look like a tennis player disappointed by the non-arrival of his partner. He threw the racket in the back of the Fiat and walked smartly towards the embassy, looking neither left nor right, a man with every legal reason to do what he was doing. He covered the sixty yards, sure that nobody was watching him. A shield with a red star and blue stripes hung above the awning. A Japanese motor-cycle was chained to the basement railings. He slipped on a pair of thin chamois-leather gloves and approached the front door at an angle that hid him from anyone at the barred windows below.

He slipped the key into the Ingersoll lock and the door swung open silently. He stood in the hallway, separating the noises in the house from those outside. The lift cage was at street level. He put his ear against the gilded grille-work and heard the faint drone of a carpet-sweeper coming from above. The door leading to the stairs was shut. So was the door to the basement. In front of him a breast-high counter split the room in two. The walls were hung with posters depicting mountain gorges straddled by electricity pylons, massed gymnastic displays performed by inscrutable-looking children, stunned peasants goggling at fleets of tractors. The sign on the counter read:

The cleaners had been and gone. The typewriters were cowled on the desks. The chairs stood in perfect alignment. The ashtrays were spotless. He used the last key on the ring and pulled the stairway door shut behind him. The street noises were suddenly stilled. He started to climb, keeping his weight close to the wall to avoid treading on creaking floor-boards. A window at the rear of the house illuminated the third-floor landing. Forty feet beneath, one of the security guards was standing on the grass in shorts, exercising. His oiled body and shaven head gleamed in the waning sunshine. There were two doors on the landing. One was open. Campbell inched forward cautiously. The buff-coloured curtains in the high-ceilinged room were drawn tight, but enough light filtered through for Campbell to see that everything was as Arbela had described it. The glass table with ivory carvings, the marble fireplace filled with dried flowers, the sofa and chairs upholstered in red plush and the coconut matting on the floor. He tiptoed across to the four-panelled screen in the left-hand corner of the room.

The safe was behind it, sunk deep into the wall, disclosing no more than an oblong surface of steel. The light was bad here but he could make out the two dials that operated the combination locks. The Frenchmen had known both the make and the model and had warned that there'd be no recesses on show. The only divergence from the flat planes were slight swellings over the concealed hinges

This was where the charges would have to go. His gloved fingers moved across the front of the safe and then stopped. He could feel a slight break in the smoothness. Then bending forward he realized the incredible truth. The safe was not locked but fractionally open. Holding his breath, he pulled the poised mass of metal towards him. The interior of the safe was divided into shelf space and a drawer. Cellophane bags were lying on their sides on the two shelves. A quick look revealed that the deep drawer was empty except for a small notebook. He held it in his hand, staring with disbelief at the cellophane bags. Slipping the mottle-covered notebook into a pocket, he weighed one of the bags in the palm of his hand. He could see the powder through the clear plastic. It looked something like soft brown sugar. The neck of the bag was tied, the string sealed with a blob of red wax bearing a dragon device. He was holding a kilo bag of heroin, the dragon device guaranteed its degree of purity.

It was two years since he had seen the stuff, sitting in the window in Mark Foy's Paris apartment, the Seine swirling around the piers below. They had been three: Mark, the man from Hong Kong and himself. The heroin on the table had been in the same sort of container, secured with the same seal. The Chinaman was a member of a Triad Society. He'd spilled a little of the odourless powder on to an upturned mirror. Mark had tested the dope with the tip of his tongue, making a face at its bitterness. The mathematics of the deal being offered were simple. The Triad's asking price was sixty thousand dollars a kilo, near-pure stuff that could be cut to as little as five per cent. Street sales in Paris and London were made in one-and-a-half-grain caps that sold for around six dollars. This meant that an investment of sixty grand could return the possibility of a million.

It was a tempting proposition but one that scared the hell out of Campbell. He'd chickened out, lacking the heart or the desire to be further involved. Two months later employees working on the Besançon sewerage farm had fished Mark Foy's head out of a tank. The rest of his body had never been found.

Cambell's eyes travelled along the shelves, counting the bags. There were six, including the one he was holding. At that moment the door leading to the adjoining room opened. The newcomer was a Korean dressed in a brown-and-white seersucker suit and wingtip shoes. He was roughly Campbell's age and equally surprised. Both men looked at each other, sharing the initial shock. The Korean was first to react, launching himself behind a lifted leg with a yell at Campbell. Campbell swung the bag of dope hard at the other man's head, catching him flush above the left ear. The Asian dropped to his knees, open mouth displaying his gold bridgework. His round pebble eyes photographed Campbell as the Canadian ran for the landing. Campbell's one thought was to get the hell out of there before the alarm was raised. He flew the stairs in three leaps and burst through the door into the hallway, stuffing his gloves in his pocket. The elevator-cage started rising as he struggled with the front door.

Then suddenly he was outside, sweating in the scented warmth of the summer evening.

He ran towards his parked car, sneaking a look back over his shoulder. He could see no sign of danger. He backed the Fiat out hurriedly, an eye on the rearview mirror as he swung into the right turn. He drove fast, not stopping till he reached the Armory in the park. He walked to the edge of the lake and stuffed the gloves down a grating. The keys he threw twenty feet out into the water. That done, he sat on a bench and tried to pull himself together.

So much for the Last Big Score, he thought. Certain facts about this caper were beyond speculation. One: he hadn't done his homework properly. According to what he had seen and heard there just shouldn't have been anyone in the Chancellery at that time. Two: someone with access to the embassy safe was bringing dope into the country, possibly smuggling it in the diplomatic bags. It had been done before. Three; the smuggler would have to be someone in a position of authority. Maybe there were more than just one. The expression on the face of the guy who'd disturbed him was evidence that the last thing they expected was a visit from a burglar. But they knew now that not only had he seen the heroin, he had actually handled it. He still figured that he was in the clear. If the Koreans decided to shift the dope and call in the law, Arbela's references were impeccable. There was no reason that he could see to associate her with the break-in.

He stretched and lighted a cigarette. The more he thought about things, the more certain he was that Arbela's information had been accurate. The trouble was that it was two weeks old. Since Arbela had seen inside the safe, the money had been replaced by heroin. And so it would go, one thing taking the place of the other till they all made millions or achieved whatever else it was that they wanted from the operation. Now he had Arbela to deal with. The news that he'd blown it was going to revive all the old familiar arguments in favour of him getting out and earning an honest living. It was almost eight o'clock. The best thing to do would be to call Arbela from home and arrange to pick her up for a late meal somewhere. A bottle of good wine drunk by candlelight would soften the news that once again his respectability would have to be postponed.

He turned the Fiat left into Pembridge Crescent. Home was in the mews that lay behind, a two-up and two-down converted from a loft and coachhouse. The ninety-nine-year lease was a bonus from the last real score he had made, a walk-in at a Belgravia birthday party. He'd raided the bedrooms while the guests were having a pre-dinner drink and had left in the guise of a London Electricity Board workman, displaying a true left-wing contempt for the butler who had let him out. Since then, his criminal forays had been meaningless, escapades that had placed him in jeopardy while hardly paying for his living expenses.

He braked, spying a free space between the linden trees. The Victorian crescent was amazingly quiet in spite of its central location, a backwater off the main stream of traffic. Dogs dozed on doorsteps.

Babies were left outside, their prams unattended. People entertained without the compulsion to lower the blinds or draw the curtains. He shifted in his seat aware of the notebook in his hip pocket. He pulled it out. It was the same size as a paperback and bound in mottled cardboard. Half the pages were covered with hieroglyphics, beautifully drawn with a fine-tipped felt pen. The script could have been Korean or for all he knew Chinese or Japanese. But whatever the content was, the book was important enough to be kept in the safe. A new idea shaped itself in his mind. Maybe there was something still to be salvaged from the expedition. The details would have to be worked out very carefully. These little yellow bastards were both tough and tricky. He peeked into the rearview mirror. The crescent was empty behind. The only person in sight was a goggled motor-cyclist thirty yards in front, bending over his machine. There was nobody to see as Campbell slipped from the car, bent low behind it and taped the notebook to the top of the fuel-tank. Paying attention to certain fundamental rules had kept him out of the slammer. The first rule was removing himself as quickly as possible from stolen property. Later on he'd find a safe place to stash the book.

He made his way towards the entrance to the mews, soaking up the familiar impressions. The stone lions that guarded the entrance to number eight, the female in the next house who always played Chopin non-stop with the loud pedal firmly depressed, the Chow dog permanently ensconced in the window-seat, baleful and vigilant. He let himself in through his front door, exchanging greetings with his neighbour. She and her husband had finally given up asking him in for drinks. Their communications were cool but courteous.

There was nothing in his house of special significance but it was his home. He had bought the furniture in a Kensington department store, so many square yards of Scandinavian schlock. The curtains and carpets were the choice of the previous tenant and had come with the lease. As Arbela said, there was no taste and little comfort but it was a refuge that he guarded jealously. Once his street door was shut he could do what he wanted without fear of interruption. It was there that he took locks to pieces and reassembled them tinkered with a jeweller's lathe, ate from cans standing up in the kitchen. Arbela had her own key. Apart from her, nobody came to the house.

He called her number from the phone in his bedroom. Her picture smiled at him out of its silver frame. It was an old picture but one that he liked, taken before her marriage to Paul Stewart, the Dartry girl from Lake Cowichan, grey-eyed, black-haired and beautiful and clearly unsure what she wanted from life. That was almost nine years ago and she still didn't seem to know what she wanted.

The engaged signal continued to sound. He cradled the phone and showered the lingering smell of fear from his body. He changed into clean slacks, a blue cotton shirt and French sneakers. He called Arbela's number again and still got the engaged signal. Her flatmate seemed to spend her upright moments talking on the phone. He decided to drive over to Rosemoor Street and collect Arbela. He'd been asked not to go to the flat. His blood got into his nose every time he saw the blonde from Saskatchewan and their conversation usually ended in mutual insults. But he could ring the bell and stay at the door.

Dragonflies were floating in the light from the overhead lamp outside. It was mealtime and the mews hummed with noise released through open windows. His feet made no sound on the cobblestones and he walked with confidence. It wasn't until he was twenty yards away from his car that his brain flashed a danger-signal. A black Mercedes with its lights out was parked facing him. Both rear doors opened as he stopped. Two figures came at him, one from each side of the limousine. He swerved away instinctively from the outstretched grabbing hands. He had a brief glimpse of the two Asian faces and recognized one of the security guards at the North Korean Embassy. The men were dressed in dark clothing and wore rope-soled shoes. A third man was sitting at the wheel of the Mercedes.

Campbell spun in his tracks, his yell of alarm splitting the quiet of the crescent. He ran scared, fear lending power to his pumping legs. By the time he reached the corner he was twenty yards up on his pursuers. Headlamps flared behind, the shadows of the men chasing him huge and grotesque in the bright light. The flat report of a silenced pistol rang out and a shell whined past his body to lose itself in the obscurity. A second shot followed. A window was thrown up and a man shouted. The headlamps grew even brighter as the Mercedes drew nearer.

Campbell's mouth was open, his head rolling, his muscles beginning to flag. He flung himself to the right despairingly, his weight bursting through the fastenings of the gate. He ran past a lighted window where people were eating, and floundered into a tangle of rhododendrons. He jumped at the ivy-draped walls, fingernails clawing for the top and purchase. For a second he dangled hopelessly. A last frantic kick carried him up and over. He lay quite still where he landed, his heart banging in his ribcage.

He stayed prone for fully five minutes, smelling the dirt and keeping his breathing shallow as if even this might betray him. Convinced at last that he'd shaken off his pursuers he picked himself up and brushed off his clothes. There were no rips or tears, no blood anywhere, but his confidence was completely shattered. Not only had someone tried to abduct him on the open street, but for the first time in his life someone had actually shot at him. Maybe they'd only meant to scare him, but the fact remained, he'd been shot at. There was no doubt in his mind what they wanted. The book he had taken had to be even more important than he imagined. And suddenly it was a whole new ballgame. He couldn't go to the police for protection. With his record they'd be waiting to throw the key away. He'd beaten them too often in the past. He could imagine the scene in the C.I.D. room as he went into his spiel. 'I was in the North Korean Embassy and there was this safe . . .' Not only that, there was Arbela to think of. Of all people she was the last who deserved to be involved. No, there had to be other ways out. As things stood it was a Mexican standoff. He couldn't go to the law but then surely nor could the Koreans. His first priority was to get the hell out of the neighbourhood in case they were still cruising it.

He'd spend the night in a small hotel, the sort of place where you put your money down in advance and no questions were asked. There were dozens of them dotted around the streets near the main railway terminals. Above all, he needed time to work things out. If they were so determined to get this notebook back it made sense to hang on to it. The book would be safe where it was. He dare not go home, at least not tonight, nor could he use his car.

He was standing in somebody's garden. The lights of the house showed through a screen of rose bushes. He picked his way through thorns, lifting his feet high. A side-door let him out into the street that ran into the crescent. He heard the man's voice as he turned the corner but it was too late to turn back. There were two of them, uniformed cops standing close to the wall. One of them was talking into a microphone clipped to his tunic. He stopped as soon as he saw Campbell, offering a hard stare that took in the Canadian's clothes and appearance.

His voice was less sure than his eyes. 'Excuse me, sir. Do you live in the neighbourhood?'

The lighted thoroughfare at the end of the street looked a thousand miles away.

'I live in the mews,' said Campbell. 'Why?' *That was it, give them the old pizazz.*

The cop took a moment to give him the benefit

22

of the doubt. 'A bit of bother, sir. I don't suppose you heard any shooting, did you?'

'*Shooting?* What kind of shooting?'

'The usual kind, sir.' The man went back to his microphone.

Campbell walked on, feeling their eyes in the small of his back. Buses were lumbering by at the end of the street. People were standing and sitting outside the pub. He crossed the street and ducked into the alleyway next to the public library. The call-box was free. He dialled Arbela's number yet again. It was two minutes to nine. This time somebody answered. He recognized the old enemy.

'It's me,' he said shortly. 'Let me talk to Arbela.'

Her voice was cool. 'Take your turn. The line forms on the right.'

He could feel the heat rising in his neck. 'What exactly is that supposed to mean?'

'That you're the third person who's asked for her in the past half-hour. She's out. She went out twenty minutes ago.'

'Went out where?'

'I've no idea.'

Campbell had established a dubious record at Canada House during the time he had been in England. There was the matter of two lost passports, the letters from his father's lawyers who were trying to trace him, confidential inquiries from Scotland Yard to the High Commissioner. Arbela's flatmate worked in the Commissioner's office, heard the gossip and disapproved of Arbela's relationship with Campbell. She made no bones about showing her feelings.

'Did she go alone?' He was doing his best to control his temper.

She made him wait before she answered, extracting the full dramatic value from her statement.

'She went out with a policeman as a matter of fact. A detective.'

It was suddenly very hot in the booth and he opened the door with a foot.

'A *detective*? What the hell would the police want with Arbela?' Hope sagged as his brain supplied the answer.

'Don't ask me,' she said pertly. 'I'd have thought you'd have known. Especially since your name came up in conversation.'

He swallowed with difficulty. The two cops he'd seen earlier were standing across the road. He turned his back on them.

'Look, Jane. I want you to cut the crap and tell me exactly what's happened to Arbela.'

'I've already told you,' she retorted. 'The man came here and asked for her by name. She was out at the laundrette. He said he was a policeman and asked if he could wait.'

'What's all this about my name coming up?'

'That was right at the beginning. He was asking if she had any boyfriends. I told him that you were the only one. He seemed pretty interested. Then when Arbela came back I left them to it. I've no idea what they were talking about or what went on. I was in my room. All I know is that when I came out she'd gone. And so had he. Look, anyway, I've got a bath running . . .'

He put the phone down and stepped out into the

alleyway. The two cops had vanished again. He lighted a cigarette nervously. His instinct not to go home was dead right. He remembered that Arbela always carried her key to his house. The police might well be there now, waiting for him. Anything was possible in this nightmare he was living.

A hotel room was out of the question now. The North Koreans must be playing it from both ends, trying to abduct him and at the same time complaining to the police. If it came to his word against theirs, what chance did he stand? He needed help, but there was no one he could trust. He needed help for himself and for Arbela. God knows what was going to happen to her. He had to find time, a breathing-space, an opportunity to think what his next move should be. Right now his brain was taking him no further than the problem of finding a place to sleep. He could think of only one place where he'd be safe until morning. He flagged down a cab that was cruising by.

'The park. You can let me off by the bridge over the Serpentine.'

He shut his eyes and tried to think. An answer slowly emerged from a welter of memories. He sat up a little straighter. There *was* a guy who could help if he could only be persuaded, someone who'd accept his story for what it was worth and be ready to tear up the rule books. The cab stopped near the bridge. He walked back past the parked cars to a telephone box on the carriageway. He used his lighter to search the directory, holding the flame over the printed entry as he dialled the number.

The engaged signal sounded. He tried the number a dozen times during the next two hours, monopolizing the booth for periods of ten minutes or more. An operator finally informed him that the phone was off the hook at the other end.

He left the box and walked across the grass. The floodlit towers at the foot of Park Lane soared in the distance. Between there and where he stood was a stretch of empty darkness. He started to walk again. There was nowhere else for him to go.

GLEN UNDERWOOD

July 19

The unmarked squad car had been parked on Wardour Street for the last twenty minutes, its front end facing north so that the two occupants had a clear view of people coming from the direction of Shaftesbury Avenue. The driver of the police car was a mousey-haired man with broken veins in his nose and ill-fitting dentures that he tended to shift with his tongue in moments of stress. He was wearing a gaudily-patterned shirt with short sleeves and wraparound sunglasses.

'The fucker's late,' he said, nodding ahead. 'Either that or he's sussed us out and isn't coming.'

'He'll be along.' Detective-Inspector Underwood spoke with confidence. He was a couple of years older than his colleague with pale brown eyes and a long narrow head. The white circle in his dark hair was the result of a childhood attack of ringworm. A silk shirt, well-tailored slacks and Gucci loafers gave him an elegance at variance with the Detective-Sergeant's vulgarity. The discrepancy was deliberate, part of the Mutt-and-Jeff act that the two men put on. Tanner's reputation on the street was that of a snake-mean cop who would arrest his own grandmother if it meant a conviction. Survivor of a disciplinary inquiry into an assault on a prisoner he still used his fists, though with more discretion. Underwood was the sympathetic listener with a manner that suggested the confessional. Over the

27

last year the two men had proved themselves the hottest team on the Drug Squad.

Underwood slid lower on his shoulderblades. 'Here he comes!'

A slim Chinese in his twenties had turned the corner. A diseased hip caused him to limp badly but he covered the ground with deceptive speed, a straw hat with a coloured band tipped forward over his eyes.

'Look at him go,' said Tanner. 'I'd like to bust his ass here and now.'

Underwood checked his watch. 'Same time as yesterday, give or take a couple of minutes.'

The driver followed the limping figure with his eyes. 'Little bastard! I'd take a chance on him, hatchet enforcer or not.'

'That's your trouble,' said Underwood. 'You're too anxious. Bust him now and you'd lose three more. We'll have Joe Yin when the moment's right and that'll mean the last of the Wo Shing Wo. The ones that matter, anyway.'

Tanner picked at a tooth. 'And no more Hong Kong brown sugar. We'll be out of business.'

'You're a dreamer, George,' said Underwood. 'The Drug Squad will never go out of business.'

A light glowed on the dash. The car was fitted with two radio sets. One, multi-channel, that operated on all the fifty police wavelengths and a radiophone for car-to-car communication.

Underwood put the receiver to his ear and heard:

'Control to Charley Delta. Detective-Inspector Underwood?'

'Speaking.'

'We have the same person back on your office line, Inspector. He won't give his name. Do you want us to lose him or not?'

'Put him on,' said Underwood.

The caller's voice was produced from high in the nose, his accent Asiatic.

'Mistah Undahwood? Impotahnt we see you immediately. You go now.'

The contact was broken. Underwood replaced the receiver, shrugging.

'One of my maggots. He wants me to meet him, something to do with a shipment. You'd better stay here. I shouldn't be long.'

Tanner nodded abstractedly, his eyes on the young Chinese girl coming towards them.

'Why is it they've all got bandy legs and no tits?'

'It's the diet,' said Underwood. 'Something to do with all that rice.'

He walked east along Gerrard Street into the heart of Chinatown, past mysterious-looking grocery stores, the bookshops and cultural centres, Hong Kong and Peking style restaurants, the illegal gambling clubs. His progress down the street was noted by slanted eyes from doorways. His nickname in the Chinese community was 'The Velvet Hammer'. There was no question there of police infiltration. It was a secret world of blackmail and tribute where fear of the Enforcer's hatchet was greater than fear of the law. Men kept their counsel rather than lose their heads.

He turned left and crossed Shaftesbury Avenue into Soho. Pignatelli's Italian Supermarket was at the end of a courtway. He entered the store, picked up a basket, collected a couple of items at random and carried them to a fire-exit. He put the basket down near the wall and walked through the door into a yard filled with dustbins. A metal staircase took him up to the third storey where a door bore a painted wooden sign:

FAR EAST NOVELTIES

He rapped on the door with his knuckles, three short, two long, three short. The door was unlocked. He stepped into a large shabbily furnished office with cartons stacked against one wall. There was a strong smell of insecticide and there were dead flies everywhere. There was a filing cabinet, a bare desk with a dusty telephone and the blinds were half-drawn. Standing near the desk was a North Korean wearing two-tone shoes and a seersucker suit.

Underwood's voice was resentful. 'I thought I'd made it absolutely clear that the number I gave you was for use in an emergency only. All those calls are recorded.'

The Korean's accent like the cut of his clothes was North American.

'This *is* an emergency.'

Underwood leaned his back against the door. He had been coming to this room for more than a year, once a month, collecting the two brown envelopes. His own always contained the same amount, eight thousand dollars in United States currency. The amount had been agreed at that first meeting, on the upper deck of a bus with rain washing the windows. He'd no idea what the other envelope contained. He merely took it to the place that Drake had specified. His paymasters varied. This was only the third time he had met Nam Cho.

'What's the problem?' Underwood asked.

Nam Cho wiped the top of the desk and perched on it. 'Do you know how many people you have arrested on my instructions, Detective-Inspector?'

Underwood cocked his narrow head. The phrase 'on my instructions' had a dangerous ring. The deal offered on top of the bus had been set up by Drake. Underwood was being paid to arrest and convict certain designated individuals, all of them Chinese. The tip-offs came in many ways, a whisper over the phone, an anonymous letter dropped through his letter-box. These supplied the evidence he needed. After nine months he had put the entire 14K Triad Society behind bars and dried up the flow of morphine-base from Amsterdam. He was now working on the other Triad Society, the Wo Shing Wo. The fact that fresh supplies of heroin were still coming into the country from somewhere did nothing to weaken the Commissioner's approval of Underwood who was clearly destined for higher things. Underwood had his own thoughts about this and kept his dollars and a false passport in a safety-deposit box.

'Twenty-six,' he said cautiously. 'Eighteen convictions, fourteen deportations and four of them voluntarily repratriated.'

Nam Cho's smile was the narrowest opening of his lips. 'How about the Wo Shing Wo?'

'Four. Joe Yin and his council go next week. Why?'

Small black eyes considered him over the slitted grin. 'A thief broke into the embassy just over two hours ago. I happened to be alone in the Chancellery. The safe in the next room was open. I heard a noise, walked through and found this man standing in front of the safe holding a bag of heroin in his hand.'

Someone flushed a toilet along the corridor. The noise sent the pigeons flapping from the windowsill. Underwood felt for a cigarette. He'd guessed what was happening months ago, that the North Koreans were putting the opposition out of business for a definite reason. But it was the first time there'd been any admission that they were importing drugs.

'You mean you kept heroin in the embassy *safe*?'

Nam Cho ignored the question. 'This man was a professional thief. He was looking for something else.'

Underwood looked down at the footmarks on the dusty floor. He had always known that sooner or later someone was going to get greedy or careless.

'So what happened?'

Nam Cho's fingers fluttered in the air. 'There was a scuffle. He dropped the bag and ran. I pressed the alarm and fortunately one of the guards has a motorcycle. He followed the man to his house.'

Underwood blew a fresh stream of smoke. 'I don't see the problem. No thief is going to run to the police even if he knows what it was that he saw. Added to that, you people have diplomatic immunity.'

'It's not what he saw,' said Nam Cho. 'He took a book with him. This book contains certain records including the names of all the people you have arrested. It's got to be recovered.'

Underwood moved to the window, a steel vice grabbing at his stomach. Flies were buzzing around the dustbins below.

'Where does the man live?'

'Pembridge Crescent Mews. There's something else. A girl has been working at the embassy as a temporary secretary. I don't propose to go into the reasons why but I'm sure that she's in on all this. I got her address from the agency.'

Underwood took the piece of paper. Arbela Stewart, 184 Rosemoor Street, S.W.3.

'She's about twenty-six or -seven,' said Nam Cho. 'Five feet eight with black hair and Canadian.'

Underwood put the paper in his pocket. 'What do you want me to do about it?'

Nam Cho's eyes were level. 'You're the expert. We already tried to grab him and failed.'

'*Grab* him?' repeated Underwood.

Nam Cho nodded. 'He's seen too much. The consequences could be disastrous. I want him found quickly.'

'But how do you know that this girl . . .' Underwood stopped, aware of the look on Nam Cho's face. 'I can question her but I'll have to turn her loose.'

Nam Cho slid from the desk. 'Let's you and I understand one another fully, Inspector. You will do exactly as you are told. The girl will know where this man is. Call me at the embassy the moment you have a lead on her. I'll give you further instructions.'

'What does this book look like?' asked Underwood.

Nam Cho measured air with his fingers. 'It's the

33

sort of thing you buy in any office supply store.'

Underwood shrugged. 'I'll do my best.'

Nam Cho smiled bleakly. 'I'm sure you will.' He opened the door leading out on to the fire escape.

Underwood made his way down, retrieved his basket in the supermarket and checked out at the cash desk. There was no sign of an embassy car in the neighbourhood, but there never was. The people he was dealing with were clever as well as dangerous. He walked back to the police car and threw the packets of pasta on the rear seat.

'We could be into something interesting.'

'Yeah?' Tanner belched and rapped himself on the breastbone. 'Christ, but I'm hungry!'

Underwood slid in beside him. 'Sixty kilos of hash are on their way from the sunny slopes of Morocco by way of Southampton. Delivery's supposed to be made next week. I've got to see someone else. I'll need the car.'

'Suits me.' Tanner yawned. 'I'll get something to eat and take in a movie. Clint Eastwood's on round the corner. I always fancied myself as Dirty Harry. Do I see you in the morning then?'

'Afternoon,' said Underwood. 'I have to go to the dentist. I wonder why it is that I have to work while you spread your ass in the movies.' He slid over into the driving seat.

Tanner poked his head back through the open window. 'To get yourself another medal, that's why.'

Underwood watched him as far as the corner of Coventry Street. His street map located Rosemoor Street just off Sloane Avenue. He picked up the radio telephone. 'Charley Delta to Control. I'm proceeding on a confidential investigation. I'll be off the air for the rest of the evening, over.'

'I read you, Charley Delta. Your message timed at twenty hours fourteen. Over and out.'

GEORGE DRAKE

July 19

He put the phone down carefully and pressed the button on the intercom. His voice betraying nothing.

'Will you come in here for a minute, Sylvia?'

He walked as far as the window. A space between two office buildings offered a narrow glimpse of St James's Park. It wasn't the fact that Kurelek had phoned that disturbed him. The association was an easy one to justify if necessary. It was Kurelek's manner that he found worrying.

Drake turned as his secretary opened the door leading to the outer office. She had come to the Yard from a clerical job with the British Museum, moved by what she called a 'wish to work for law and order'. Drake had his own views on the real reason for the move. She was thirty-five and unmarried and the ratio of men to women at Scotland Yard was six to one. However she was discreet, devoted and diligent and had been with him since his appointment to the rank of Commander.

She stood in the doorway anxious-eyed and wearing flat heels with a striped cotton dress.

'I've got to go out for a couple of hours,' he said. 'There's nothing in the works that can't wait, is there?'

She glanced down at the book she was holding and shook her head.

'There's Detective-Superintendent Reardon of C

Division. He's coming at three o'clock. That's the Baker case.'

He nodded. Reardon was one of the old school with none of this Police College bullshit about him. And clipjoints like the *Late Night Final* had been going for years, traps for businessmen and tourists who deserved what they got. These places were staffed by waiters who were short-change artists, sold champagne at £40 a bottle and had the best-looking hookers in the business. There was something funny about charging a man like Baker with 'living on the immoral earnings of prostitutes'. The hookers who worked for him were already hiring lawyers, incensed at the implied lack of respect for their profession. Baker had had his chance to join the club back in the old days, but he'd refused. So he was going to have to learn the hard way that you just don't buck the system.

'Make an appointment for Reardon with Sands,' said Drake. 'There wasn't anything else, was there?'

His secretary's manner indicated that there was. There was no hair in her eyes but she made the vague brushing movement that never failed to irritate him. Better she saved the coyness for the Merton Park Tennis Club dances.

She smiled uncertainly. 'Mrs Drake left a message. She wanted you to remember that cat food.'

He leaked a sarcastic smile. Afternoon sunshine flooded the room, brightening the carpet and furniture. His blue serge suit was shabby and his tie spotted with soup stains.

'Yes, well,' he said. 'That's life, isn't it? Here we are doing our best to protect society from muggers and thieves and Mrs Drake's got nothing better to do than worry about cat food. Send someone out for the stuff. With any luck it'll choke the bugger.'

Her quick smile was appreciative. 'Will you be back this afternoon, Commander?'

There was no handle on the outside of the door leading to the corridor. A spring lock fastened it.

'I'm not sure,' he answered. 'But there's no need for you to wait. Leave the cat food on my desk.'

He travelled by Underground, surfacing at White City station and walking north past the B.B.C. studios and the greyhound stadium, on past the vandalized territory surrounding the highrise council flats as far as the corner of Ducane Road. The traffic slowed and he lumbered across to the opposite pavement and loosened his belt, breathing heavily. He wasn't getting enough exercise.

Five minutes more took him into a neighbourhood of used car dealers, factory areas spiked with guard dog warnings and the slopes of railway embankments. The premises he was looking for were immediately ahead. A high barbed-wire fence enclosed ten acres of broken machinery, coils of copper wire and stacks of rusting iron. A compressing machine controlled from a crane was moulding junked cars into bales of scrap metal. He gave his name to the security guard on the gate and made his way up the path to the red-brick building. A modest sign planted in the grass read

GEORGE KURULEK LTD
CASH BUYERS OF ALL FERROUS AND NON-FERROUS
METALS FACTORY DEMOLISHERS AND DISMANTLERS

He opened a door. A girl in a striped cotton dress looked up from her desk.

'Commander Drake? Would you come this way, please. Mr Kurulek is expecting you.'

Which would be the understatement of the week, he thought. He followed her through an open plan office area to a cork-lined door marked *Private*. She rapped on it gently with her knuckles, threw it wide and smiled. She closed the door quietly behind him. All she needed was to make a curtsey. The sunny room was the key to an interior decorator's idea of what an 'executive suite' should look like in the seventies. French windows opened on to an enclosed courtyard with a pergola and plants. The walls were decorated with *trompe-l'œil* scenes of the Alhambra. A glass and chrome desk and chair unit was mounted on an electrically controlled turntable. Dali prints hung on the flocked walls and the carpet was Persian. Drake had seen it before and was not impressed.

The man waiting for him was built like a wrestler, his heavy torso tastefully draped in a bottle green silk suit. He wore his hair with a low old-fashioned side parting. It's uncompromising whiteness was accentuated by wild black eyebrows. Kurulek pushed out his hand, drawing Drake towards him slightly as the Commander gripped it.

His English was easy but delivered with a strong Central European accent.

'For the record, you are here on official business. We have been losing gold in the smelting furnace. This is true. Scraping soot from bloody chimneys. No such thing as honesty, Commander.'

Drake retrieved his hand, shaking his head at Kurelek's offer of a drink. The bar was concealed behind a panel of black glass. It was ironical that Kurulek should have the right to handle gold. Licences to smelt precious metals were issued only after extensive enquiries. Kurulek had held a licence for more than ten years. But then few people knew of his antecedents. He had no police record. The popular story was that he'd arrived in England from Hungary after the uprising of November 1956, one of four thousand anti-communist students who were given political asylum. The truth was that he'd hitched a ride with his betters, a twenty-year-old stateless rogue with fifteen carats of river quality diamonds concealed in an anal suppository. An Interpol warrant for Kurulek's arrest followed two years later. His defence to the charge of murder and theft brought at the Extradition hearing had succeeded and he'd been released. He'd come a long way since then. With no apparent chink in his own armour, he found gaping holes in that of others. His *tour-de-force* was the unasked-for favour granted, the gratuitous generosity that concealed the whiplash of a cobra. Drake knew him well and had been blocking Kurulek's overtures for a dozen years. But he always listened, cautious and aware, profiting wherever he could. Kurulek shut the glass-fronted bar. 'All the years we've known one another you've never trusted me, right?'

'Right,' said Drake.

Kurulek turned, his grin leaving a lot of air between his teeth. 'Suppose I gave a little whisper in your ear, Commander. About a couple of Italians with the plates for forging twenty dollar bills. What would you do?'

Drake's face was stony. 'I'd have someone take a good look inside my ear for a start. Then I'd ask myself for a motive. Why's he doing it? What does he want from me?'

Kurulek glanced down at his crocodile shoes. 'The answer to that is self-preservation. In any case, I'm giving not taking.'

'That's exactly what makes my toes curl,' said Drake.

Kurulek's head lifted. 'Two men are flying into Heathrow from Milan next Thursday. They'll be checking into the Hilton Hotel using the names Szabo and Graziani. One of the bags they'll be carrying will have a false bottom. That's where the plates will be. They'll also be carrying specimen twenty dollar bills made with the plates.'

The sunshine was bright in the patio, bright enough for the *trompe l'œil* scenes of Granada. Drake cracked a knuckle thoughtfully.

It would be Kurulek who had set up the deal, betraying his associates in some involved bid for power or position.

'You mean you're asking for nothing in return?' Drake's voice was frankly disbelieving.

Kurulek shook his head. 'Bury them! That's all I ask. Throw away the key! Thursday, *Alitalia*. Don't forget. There's only one flight from Milan. They'll be on their toes so I wouldn't hang about if I were you. And if you need a holding charge, they'll be travelling on false passports.'

It was after five by the time Drake arrived back

41

at the Yard but the Assistant Commissioner in charge of C Division was still in his office. Lieutenant-Colonel Grandy, O.B.E., had come to the police by way of a motorized cavalry regiment. He was wearing a blue flannel suit with a rosebud in the jacket lapel and a moustache on the order of those worn by Douglas Fairbanks and the late Errol Flynn. His eyes bulged like a cod's, his hair was carefully placed and his voice seemed to be produced through a mouthful of Plovdi plums.

'Now then, George. You wanted to see me?'

He shot a keen look from Drake's face to the desk. The basket was filled with papers. The inkwell was fashioned from a horse's hoof. A framed picture of Grandy winning the Military Trophy hunter-chase hung on the wall behind the desk.

Drake spoke his piece and Grandy whistled. 'I like it, George. I like it a lot. Your contacts never cease to amaze me. God knows where you manage to get hold of them.'

Drake's features assumed a look of zeal. 'I thought I'd better bring it direct to you, sir. Especially since the Americans are involved. It's their currency the Italians are forging.'

'Quite right,' Grandy said heartily. Bandy Grandy, the cavalryman, ready to share his blanket and meal with one of his troopers. 'I know better than to ask a man for the source of his information, but how strong is this stuff? Reliable, is it?'

Drake lifted a shoulder. 'When I'm dealing with villains I'm sure, but I'm never certain. The way I see it, sir, is what do we have to lose?'

'Right again!' Grandy bounced a couple of steps

and spoke into the intercom. 'Get me the duty officer at the American Embassy.'

Drake's voice was respectful. 'I'll leave it with you, then, sir, shall I?'

Grandy's head was cocked, listening to some far off bugle call. 'What? Oh yes, George. I'll handle this one myself. In any case it's not your line of country any more, is it?'

'No, sir.'

Grandy's interest in his subordinate was rapidly diminishing. 'But you'll get the credit that's due, of course. How long is it to retirement by the way?'

'Just over twenty months, sir.'

'Good work,' Grandy said heartily. 'And what better than another commendation on your Two-Five-Eight. You've had a good innings, George. Come a long way from wearing out shoe leather in Southwark.'

Drake smiled dutifully. A long way for a snotnose with his ass hanging out of his trousers. A long way for someone who was twelve years old before he could read or write.

'I've just had the luck to be part of the best police force in the world, sir.' It was a good mixture of modesty and achievement.

A voice spoke from the intercom. 'The American Embassy, Commissioner.'

Grandy's fingers fluttered dismissal and Drake stepped out into the corridor. He was biding his time as he'd done for years. Grandy stood for everything that Drake loathed and feared. It was good to sock it to the fucker, all the while looking bug-eyed with sincerity.

ARBELA STEWART

July 19

The afternoon sunshine flooding into the room struck fire from the beeches at the far end of the garden. She switched off her typewriter, covered it with a hood and took her handbag from a drawer. The small hand mirror showed a wide mouth and grey eyes. People said that she looked like her father, but the resemblance was difficult for her to accept. Her shoulder-length hair was the same colour as her mother's, a peat brown so dark that it was almost black. The shape of her mouth was her mother's, alive and ready to laugh. Only in her eyes was a hint of what people meant, a directness of look that came from her father.

She was wearing a pale green, linen dress with short sleeves and sandals on her bare feet. Her only jewellery was the small bracelet watch. Her wedding ring, with the rest of her trinkets, was in a box under her bed. She put her lipstick and mirror back in her bag. The henna-rinsed woman she worked with had already gone home. It was twenty minutes past five. Arbela had started staying late ten days ago, pleading unfinished work as an excuse. She had taken advantage of the time spent alone in the chancellery to make the key impressions that Roddy had asked for. It hadn't been easy. She was nervous and the cuttle-bone kept breaking and the keys were kept in the First Secretary's desk. It had taken almost a week before she finally succeeded. Now she stayed on late because Roddy had told her she must. Her pattern of behaviour had to remain the same. Her job finished on the following Friday. She was in her fifth week, deputizing for the two permanent secretaries while they were away on summer vacation. The agency she used specialized in temporary jobs paying top money. The advantage was that if the jobs proved dull or downright unpleasant at least they didn't last long.

The second day she had worked at the embassy she'd gone to a King's Road café for lunch. Chelsea was only ten minutes' walk away. She'd returned from lunch a quarter of an hour early to find no one else in the Chancellery. The door to the Ambassador's private office was open, but she had no way of knowing whether or not this was normal procedure. She was reading at her desk when she heard the unmistakable sound of someone walking on the coconut matting. Looking up, she'd seen the First Secretary standing in front of the open safe. He was facing the window with his profile to her. She could see past him into the safe. The shelves were crowded with stacks of neatly packed money. It was impossible to determine the country of origin or the denomination. Nam Cho had turned very slowly as though sensing her look, his expression impassive as their eyes met. Then walking forward, he'd closed the door between them. A short while later she heard the sound of the lift, whether going up or down she was unable to tell.

She sat for a moment, uncertain what to do or say. It was obvious to her that Nam Cho had been taken by surprise. He couldn't have known that she was in the outer office. She felt vaguely guilty, as if she'd committed some sort of gross indiscretion without knowing what. She'd picked up some work from the desk, a set of statistics that needed processing. The reaction was unthinking, a token justification for her presence there. The adding machine was kept on a stand near the window. Looking down she saw the previous printout still hanging where the last user of the machine had left it. The columns of figures were expressed in terms of U.S. dollars. The total read:

$$\$428,085.00$$

She left quickly, spending the next ten minutes in the cloak room. When she returned, the printout had disappeared. She did her best for the rest of the afternoon to put the incident out of her mind, but the task proved impossible. Two things were clear. There was a great deal of money in the embassy safe and she wasn't supposed to know about it.

What followed she took as an example of her inability to learn from experience. She'd told Roddy what she had seen. What kind of fool could she have been, imagining that he was going to change his life style for her? They'd been locked in the same stale bitter argument for more than three years. It was almost as though the business about the safe and its contents was an excuse to challenge his intentions once and for all, to put an end to his string of broken promises.

She looked at her watch again and the door to the Ambassador's private room opened. Three years at Harvard had given Nam Cho an American accent and a taste for light-coloured summer suits. He glanced across at the clock, giving her his courteous oblique smile.

'It's almost half past five, Mrs Stewart. I'm going to have to lock up. You can leave whatever it is you are doing till tomorrow morning.'

He was invariably polite to her yet he made her feel nervous. Looking at him, she thought, was like looking at a cat that anticipates every move that you make. She put the unsigned letters in the OUT tray and picked up her bag.

'I'm on my way.'

He nodded without bothering to glance in her direction. Not once since the all-important day had she seen the safe open.

'How much longer do you have with us, Mrs Stewart?'

He was at the window now, looking down into the garden, his back still towards her.

'I finish on the thirtieth,' she said.

He turned now and faced her. 'If you need a reference I shall be glad to supply you with one.'

She rose, dark hair swinging. Even in sandals she was inches taller than he was.

'I'm glad my work has been satisfactory.'

There was a feeling of peace once outside. The orderly square and well-kept gardens basked in the sunshine. It was worrying to remember that in less than an hour Roddy would be breaking into the house she'd just left. He told her no more than was necessary, but there were certain things that she had to know. She realized that complicity was something she was going to have to learn to live with. She couldn't have it both ways. Roddy had insisted that the robbery must be done while she was still employed at the embassy. If they waited till she left, he said, suspicion would fall on her.

It was a quarter to six when she turned on to Rosemoor Street. The eight flats in her building were leased to people who were out at work all day and her present job meant that she was always first home. She let herself into her flat, bending down and picking up the post. There was nothing for her, which was hardly surprising. Apart from bills, she rarely received any letters. She hadn't written home in five years and there was nobody else to correspond with. Her small rented flat was typical of its kind in the neighbourhood. Two bedrooms and a sitting room with faded chintz covers concealing worn sofas and chairs. She had found the place shortly after landing in England. Signing the tenancy agreement had been the first mark of her independence from Roddy. By that time she knew she was in love with him but it was an emotional area cluttered with memories and hang-ups. She would sleep with him, yes. But she would neither live with nor marry him until he started to earn an honest living. She'd no intention of spending the rest of her life waiting for monthly visiting-privileges to some prison or other. Once was enough, playing those rules.

It was Monday and her flatmate worked late at Canada House. She wouldn't be home till seven at the earliest. Arbela showered and washed her hair. It always gave her confidence. Dressed again, she did the chores, trying to forget what was happening in the North Korean Embassy. Her flatmate's breakfast things were still in the sink. Arbela washed them, sick of Jane Hope in the way one gets sick of a woman who never makes a mistake. It would be a relief to get back to Canada. It didn't really matter if it wasn't to that dream house Roddy was always talking about, the horses and salmon streams up in the Big Country. She ran the carpet-sweeper for twenty minutes and watered the collection of houseplants. Her bedroom was small with just enough space for a single bed, dressing-table and wardrobe. A snapshot of Roddy Campbell was tucked into the frame of the oval mirror. She lifted the lid of her dirty linen-basket. It was full. If she took the clothes now, the laundrette would be empty. She could start the machine and do her shopping in the supermarket. She emptied the basket into a plastic container. Half an hour later she was sitting in front of the washing machine, watching the sodden mass of clothing revolve. It was a slow cycle and she read her magazine, in no hurry to return to Rosemoor Street. The last few days had been torture and at the back of her mind she was dreading the call from Roddy. She put the laundry through the dryer and walked east to the supermarket. It was twenty to nine by the Town Hall clock as she crossed King's Road to go home.

She was putting her key in the lock when she heard the man's voice inside the flat. He was standing in the living room, a man of forty-five or so, smartly dressed in slacks and a silk shirt. He had a long thin face, snapping eyes and a disc of white on the side of his head. Her first feeling was one of irritation. It was an established house rule that men-friends never came to the flat. The rule had been instituted because of Roddy and Jane's intense dislike for one another. Her anger abated as she took in her flatmate's old stained bathrobe, the wet blonde hair snatched up in a towel. Jane couldn't have been expecting her visitor or she would never have been caught like that.

The man cocked his thin head like an alert collie. He seemed perfectly at home.

'Mrs Stewart?'

'Yes,' she replied. She was at the airing cupboard, the still-damp clothing trailing from her hand. It wasn't so much that he knew her name but the way he said it that surprised her. She looked past him to her flatmate who lifted her shoulders unhelpfully.

'I'm a police officer,' he said. 'I understand that you know a Mr Roderic Campbell.'

'That's right,' she said. Her blood had run cold but she continued pushing the clothing on to the drying rack.

He turned to her flatmate, the abrupt gesture adding weight to his request.

'If you don't mind, miss. This is a personal matter and I'd like a few words alone with Mrs Stewart.'

Jane closed her bedroom door on them. The living room was quiet except for the buzz of the hair-dryer coming from the neighbouring room. Arbela fished a cigarette from the packet on the table. The police officer struck a match for her deftly. Then before she could stop him, he was rummaging through her purse. He opened her address book, smiling as he leafed through the entries.

'R. Campbell. Pembridge Crescent Mews.'

She grabbed at the book, her face flaming. He skipped back holding the address book just out of reach.

'Take it easy, Mrs Stewart. We don't want more trouble than we already have.'

He dipped into her purse, still watching her carefully and found the two keyrings. He tried one set on the front door and it fitted. He held the other high in the air, grinning.

'And this one?'

She said nothing, the blood pouring into her face again. He shook his head from side to side.

'I'm going to have to ask you to come with me, Mrs Stewart.'

She cast her eyes round the room, seeking reassurance. This had to be happening to someone else. The man gave her back her purse, retaining the keys.

'Shouldn't I be allowed to call a lawyer?' she said hesitantly. She'd no idea which lawyer. Her only thought was that Roddy must have been arrested.

The question seemed to surprise him and he frowned. 'A *lawyer*? Come on now, Mrs Stewart, you've been watching too much television. This is a simple, routine inquiry and nothing else.'

She tried to see beyond the smooth easy manner and failed. 'You mean I'm not accused of some crime?'

'Don't be dramatic!' He held the door open for her. His car was parked in Sloane Avenue. Still polite, he handed her into the passenger seat. His manner was almost friendly now. He smiled re-

51

assuringly through the windshield as he made his
way round the front of the car. There was a radio-
phone on the shelf under the dash, a buff envelope
with *New Scotland Yard* printed on it.

He climbed in beside her. 'It won't take long.
Just a few questions and we'll have you back home.
There's nothing at all to worry about.'

JOHN RAVEN

July 20

Viewed from Battersea Bridge, he thought, the *Albatross* looked more elegant than she did at close quarters even after all the hard work he'd put in that summer. He'd spent three weeks, hanging over the side in a home-made harness, enduring the ribaldries of passing boatmen, painting the hull down as far as the waterline. The one clearly un-aesthetic note was the line of washing that Mrs Burrows insisted on draping across the deck.

The evening with Jerry Soo had done him a lot of good and he'd been thinking about their coming trip to the South Tyrol. Jerry skiied in a flamboyant style, close to the ground even when on the flat with a lot of energetic pole-work. It would be the fifth year running that they'd gone off somewhere together and, looking back, Louise showed a lot of style in bowing out. It was an area that, though certainly not barred to her, might have been mined.

He jogged the last few hundred yards of his daily mile, six feet three inches tall, his gangling height exaggerated by brief running shorts. His blue T-shirt was mapped with bleach-stains. The gangway leading on to the houseboat was attached to the masonry with a locked door at the end. The coils of barbed wire had been placed there to discourage unwelcome visitors. Back in the old days disgruntled customers had tried their hands at arson and burglary. Across the street was his local pub, next to it the Herborium. The establishment was owned by his neighbour who allowed Raven to park in the alleyway.

He ducked under the line of wet socks and underpants that Mrs Burrows insisted on washing herself. She held that the laundry didn't exist that took proper care of such articles. He unfastened the starboard door to the sitting room. The bright sunshine sought out the mends and the darns in the Aubusson, varnished the blacks and the blues of his treasured Klee. The six walnut chairs and table had belonged to his dead parents. They were the only things on the boat that had come from the old house in Suffolk. The rest was in store or with Anne. His sister needed the stuff more than he did. It was fair comment to say that marriage to a teacher of economics hadn't improved her finances. The long room was spotless, brass and silver polished, the surfaces dusted. The only sign of disorder was on the shelves that housed his record collection. He'd already catalogued four hundred and seven of them and as many were waiting. Mrs Burrows's idea of cleaning dust from a record was with a wet dishcloth and the shelves were off-limits to her.

His daily help caught him halfway to his bedroom, filling the kitchen doorway with her ample frame. She was a short woman of sixty-six with soft white hair and a misleading appearance of gentleness. She had gained weight during the last year and the floral apron she was wearing did nothing to disguise the fact. She looked Raven up and down with frank disapproval.

'No wonder you complain that they whistle at you! Gallivanting about like that dressed like a schoolboy at your age! You're getting as bad as him next door.'

The reference was to his neighbour. There wasn't a scrap of evidence to suggest that Saul Belasus was anything but disinterested in sex, yet in Mrs Burrows's mind the owner of the Herborium was the essence of lechery and lewd behaviour. She worked for Raven three hours every morning, five days a week. After seven years of it he was used to the cut-and-thrust of their conversation.

'You could do with a little exercise yourself,' he suggested mildly. 'All that Guinness is beginning to show.'

There was a strong smell of *chili-con-carne*. Born in Battersea, not a mile from where the *Albatross* was moored, Mrs Burrows had never travelled further in her life than Brighton. She fed her husband on fish-and-chips four nights a week. The previous Christmas she had presented Raven with a copy of *How to Cook One Hundred National Dishes*. Using her gift as a guide, she started preparing meals for her employer. She had already worked her way through the book, from Abyssinia to Zaire and was now on her second circuit. Raven ate few of her offerings, feeding them to the fish and the gulls after she'd gone.

Mrs Burrows bridled. 'You've no call to worry about *my* weight, Mr Raven. Why there still isn't enough flesh on you to feed a spadger. It's a waste of time cooking for you, preparing all them lovely meals. I don't know why I bother.'

He cocked his head. 'Perhaps it's because you love me.'

'Love you!' She snorted contemptuously. 'There isn't a man worth the bleedin' misery. Though come to think of it, I'd have done a better job on you than all them la-di-da hussies you waste your time with. *And* there wouldn't have been any of that smutty talk I've had to listen to on this boat in me time.'

'No smutty talk, Mrs Burrows.' He shook his head, his face serious.

'Well,' she said. 'Your food's in the oven. You can warm it up whenever you like. I'm off.'

She took her apron off and slammed it into a drawer. 'There's a man been phoning all morning. He says it's important and I should bleedin' well hope so. Five times at least I had to stop me work and run and answer. "He's out," I says. "But you must have some idea when he'll be back," he says. Which shows he can't be a friend of yourn or he'd have known better.'

Raven dislodged the fly that had landed on his sweaty neck. 'Did he leave his name?'

'He did not,' she said. 'Very secret he was. Not that he sounded like Scotland Yard.'

She steadfastly refused to believe in Raven's resignation from the Force, preferring to think that this was no more than a clever ruse to conceal his undercover work.

'But he must have left a number,' he said patiently.

'That he did,' she said. She jerked a thumb at the baize-topped games table. 'It's under your horse.'

The small bronze he had found in Greece was pinning down a piece of paper.

'I'm off,' she repeated. 'He's a Yank, I can tell

you that much. You're supposed to be ringing him at twelve o'clock sharp if you're in and you *are* in. Give me me money.'

She was an inveterate backer of indifferent horses and liked to be paid daily. He gave her the sum that he owed and heard her slam the gangway door. The smell of chili permeated through the boat. He tipped the contents of the pan into a plastic bag and dropped it over the side. The fish probably had stronger digestions than he had.

One of these days he would have to break the news to Mrs Burrows.

It was after eleven by the pigskin travelling clock at his bedside. The electric fan discouraged the mosquitoes that had swarmed on the river that summer. He'd recently bought himself a portable colour television. The stand was installed at the foot of his bed. His sister sneered at it, but the truth was it was better than evenings spent with the radical chic of Hampstead and he did include his brother-in-law.

He took a cold shower, put on cotton slacks, a short-sleeved shirt and sandals. His hair was definitely getting thinner. The girl who did it suggested cutting it shorter but it was staying the length it was. It no longer annoyed people and he liked it that way. He put a recording of Handel's *Messiah* on the player and poured himself a pint of cold *Budweiser*. He could think of no American who'd be likely to call him. He took the beer out on deck, keeping an eye through the window on his bedroom clock. It was too hot to wear a watch. At twelve exactly he called the number on the piece of paper in front of him.

The response was immediate, the man's voice low and guarded. It sounded as if his hand was cupped round the mouthpiece.

'John Raven,' said Raven.

'Do you know who this is?' the voice asked quietly.

There was just enough said to be able to fit a face to the whisper.

'I do,' said Raven. 'It's Roddy Campbell. What do you want? I'd have thought you'd have done us all a favour by now and gone back to Canada.'

'I'm in trouble. Bad trouble. I need your help.'

Raven turned down the volume on the record-player. 'Did you say you need my help?'

'Yes. I'm on the level, Raven.'

Raven stretched his long spindly legs. 'I'm not surprised to hear you're in trouble, but what do you want me to do about it? There's nothing I can do for you. I've been off the Force for over three years.'

'I know it.' The Canadian's voice was urgent. 'But you can still help me. Look, Raven, I'm not bull-shitting. A couple of people look like getting hurt and I'm one of them.'

It was the fear in the other man's voice that en-gaged Raven's curiosity. The likable rogue he remembered hadn't scared that easily. He was a jewel-thief in the old tradition who used audacity and his brains instead of a sawn-off shotgun.

'I don't understand what you're trying to tell me,' said Raven.

'I can't tell you now, not over the phone. You'll have to come here. It'll work two ways, Raven. Help me and I'll put you on to something that's really big. Something that'll take the lid off the drug scene here.'

Raven had carried the phone to the end of the cord. A pigeon planed down on the deck near his foot. He lunged but missed.

'I don't have very happy memories of you, you know,' he said. 'You made me look a real Charley.'

'That's history, for God's sake!' A touch of despair crept into Campbell's tone. 'There's a girl's life involved. Can you hear me, Raven?'

'I heard you, A girl's life's involved.'

'Someone fired two shots at me on the street last night.'

'I'm waiting for the violins,' said Raven. The pigeon was on the next boat, preening its feathers. The Great Dane took no notice of it.

'I thought you had more intelligence than that,' said Campbell. 'But if that's the way it has to be . . .'

'Hold it,' said Raven. It was ironic that of all people Campbell should come to him for help. 'Where are you speaking from?'

'I'm in a call-box in Hyde Park, near Forte's restaurant. It's about three hundred yards up coming from Knightsbridge. I'll be on the grass behind.

'Twenty minutes,' promised Raven. He finished the last of his beer, took the record off the machine and locked up the houseboat. His insurance premiums had decreased since he had become a member of the general public, it was a comment on morals that he still didn't fully appreciate.

He had changed his car in June, remaining faithful to the French. His current choice was a Citroën, a silver Pallas with dark blue jersey interior. He drove into the park, leaving the car in the restaurant forecourt and walking back across the grass. Workers in the neighbouring stores and offices were taking their lunchtime breaks in the sun, some of them eating the food they had brought along. A Red Setter, soaked from a swim in the Serpentine, shook itself vigorously, showering Raven. It's mistress smiled indulgently. A man lying in the shadow of a beech tree removed the newspaper from his face as Raven drew near. Raven sat down beside him.

'It's been a long time. How are you?'

The Canadian's clothes were respectable enough. It was his face that looked odd, cheeks sprouting a reddish stubble, his eyes bleary and tired-looking. Other than that the years seemed to have treated him leniently. He struggled upright, the vein in his forehead distended.

'You can skip the chat. You're not selling life insurance.'

Raven blinked. 'Correct me if I am wrong, but I had the idea you were asking for my help.'

'I am.' Campbell shook his ginger head. 'I'm sorry. Too much has happened the last few hours.'

Raven stuck a blade of grass in his mouth. 'This may come as a shock, but there's something you're going to have to tell me before we go another yard. Are you with me?'

Campbell's eyes narrowed. He had the fair skin

that went with his colouring and the creases were deep in his freckled face.

'I'm no good at riddles.'

Raven explained. The last time they had met had been in the lobby of a Belgrave Square apartment-block. A hurricane of jewel-thefts had hit the area. The Serious Crimes Squad in the person of Raven was assigned the job of apprehending the culprits. The methods employed, the nature and scope of the targets, had been fed into the police computer. The iron brain had come up with half a dozen suspects. The name Raven liked best was Campbell's. He baited his traps, staking out half a dozen blocks of flats in the area. The staffs, male and female, had been replaced by officers under Raven's command. Raven himself had roamed the district in his car, never far from the scene of action, allowing himself no more than the bare time to eat and sleep.

Campbell struck within the week. His arrival was reported to Raven by radiophone and the Canadian was allowed to proceed unchallenged. All secondary entrances to Surrey House were closed. Raven stationed himself in the lobby. Once he reached the fifth floor Campbell appeared to vanish through solid wall. Ten minutes later he stepped out of an elevator in the lobby. Questioned, he claimed to be looking for a Mrs Rowena Grice, a one-time tenant of a flat in the block. He was taken to the manager's office, stripped and then searched. Nothing incriminating was found on his person. He used the next five minutes to harangue Raven about the hazards of making false arrests and left on the same note. Two hours later, a Mrs Feinglass

DONALD MACKENZIE

returned to her fifth-floor flat to reappear in the lobby in a state of collapse. During her brief absence someone had removed fifty-seven thousand pounds worth of jewellery from her bedroom.

'I want to know what you did with it,' said Raven.

Cambell's look was embarrassed. 'You don't really expect me to answer a question like that!'

Raven switched the blade of grass from one side of his mouth to the other.

'I was never more serious.'

'That's great,' said Campbell, shaking his head. 'What you're doing here is asking me to put my head on the chopping-block. I could get five for that job. It's blackmail.'

'Bullshit,' said Raven. 'It's an academic exercise. I'm not a cop any longer and I don't give a fuck about Mrs Feinglass, her jewellery *or* the insurance company. I'm only interested in knowing how you made a fool out of me. Call me a bad loser if you like.'

Campbell raised a hand. 'O.K., O.K.! The windows on the south side of that building overlook West Halkin Street, right?'

'Right,' said Raven.

'My car was under the bedroom with the top down. I put the gear in a holdall. Keys, loot and gloves. Then I dropped it out of the window.'

The simplicity of the explanation needled Raven, but he felt like a man who has just had an aching tooth pulled.

'You mean you knew that we were there?'

'I figured you would be,' said Campbell. 'I tried to think as you would. It wasn't too difficult. It was always touch and go between you and me. It could have gone either way on a couple of occasions.'

Raven eased his feet out of the sandals. 'Suppose I'd walked round the corner and noticed this convertible?'

'Among six other cars?' Campbell shrugged. 'The point is that you didn't. The only risk I ran was some other bastard nicking the bag before I got there.'

Raven moved his head up and down. 'O.K. You paid your dues. I'm ready to listen.'

He heard Campbell out, never interrupting, assessing both the tale and the way it was told.

'Do you know what this sounds like to me?' he said at the end. 'It sounds like some kind of a con. My toes have been curling for the last quarter of an hour and that's always a bad sign.'

Campbell waited for a couple of lovers to pass. 'A con, is it?'

'It's a little heavy,' said Raven. 'You've got to admit.'

Campbell's voice was bitter. 'What kind of a clown do you take me for? Every single word I've said is the truth. I respected you, Raven, but something's happened. You've turned into a phoney.'

'Wrong,' Raven said cheerfully. 'It's just that you've outsmarted me once. I'm trying to make sure that you don't do it again. How did you come to meet this girl in the first place?'

'Her husband was a good friend of mine. We were at school together. After that we worked together. You know. Till some trigger-happy farmer blew Paul's brainpan apart. I was there when it happened. I had to break the news to his wife. A couple of months afterwards I brought her to Europe. I'd always been in love with her. I still am.'

An ant was crawling over Raven's ankle. He waited till it left his skin. People used the word 'love' to justify otherwise indefensible actions, including murder.

'It sounds as though the lady has a great future,' he said.

Campbell's freckled face was defiant. 'What the hell do you know about it? Arbela's straight. She's always been straight, even with Paul. She'd no idea where the money was coming from. She thought he was some kind of salesman.'

The parched grass about them smelled like a hayfield. Raven's nostrils narrowed.

'What I'm saying is that you have a strange way of showing your affection. Didn't it occur to you that you'd be involving her in all this?'

Campbell flushed, he was obviously offended. 'Yes, it occurred to me. But I was trying to take her out of this goddam country. To give her the kind of life she deserves. And I don't need your moralizing. I read my newspapers and no woman ever killed herself because of me.'

It was a low blow and dirty and because of that hurt all the more. But Cathy had killed herself and the coroner's assessment of her reasons had made the headlines. The fact that he was wrong was beside the point.

'Suppose we stop insulting one another,' Raven suggested quietly. 'I'm sorry if I needled you. You say you slept in the park?'

The flush faded from Campbell's face. 'You don't

sleep in a park, friend. In any case there were a number of things to think about.'

'I can imagine,' said Raven.

'You still think I'm lying, don't you?' Campbell challenged.

Raven pushed the hair out of his eyes. 'I'm not sure,' he said truthfully.

There was a hint of defeat in the Canadian's voice. 'Well, it's up to you, isn't it? I've told you all there is to tell. The car's in Pembridge Crescent and the book should still be taped to the fuel tank.'

Raven slipped his feet into his sandals. 'I'd like a little wander before I make up my mind.'

Campbell's hand shot out, grabbing Raven's sleeve. 'I want to know now, one way or another. If your answer's no then I'll have to start thinking again. It isn't just for me. It's Arbela I'm scared for. I've got a hunch that guy wasn't a cop at all.'

Raven freed his arm carefully. 'Why?' The suspicion had been in his own mind ever since he'd heard, but he wanted to know the other man's reasons.

Campbell emphasized them on his fingers. 'I've been thinking about it all night. Cops are like crows. They usually travel in pairs. This one didn't, right? Here's another thing. Why didn't he give his name or rank. But the way I see it, the most important reason for thinking this guy's a phoney is that the Koreans just can't *afford* to go to the police.'

'I agree,' said Raven and climbed to his feet. He held out his hand. 'I'll take the keys to your house and your car.'

Campbell dropped them into Raven's palm. 'It's

number eight Pembridge Crescent Mews, a house with a yellow door. You'll find the car parked just round the corner, a Fiat. QM 6196. Does this mean you're definitely with me?'

'That's what it means,' said Raven. 'Are you all right for money?'

'Thirty or forty pounds,' said Campbell.

'Then get yourself shaved,' said Raven. 'Have a meal and then hide yourself in a movie. There are plenty in the area. I'll be back here at eight o'clock sharp and we'll find you a bed for the night.'

When he looked back, Campbell was already making his way across the grass, heading in the direction of Knightsbridge. It was after one by the time Raven reached Pembridge Crescent. He stayed in the car, getting a feel of the place. It was a green and shady neighbourhood, a haven in the encroaching sleaziness of Notting Hill Gate and Westbourne Grove, an establishment stronghold that was bound to be under the frequent surveillance of the police. Campbell's claim was that he hadn't turned a trick in a year but the money had to be coming from somewhere. This was an expensive area to live in.

The Canadian's small black Fiat was visible twenty yards ahead, the two nearside wheels up on the pavement. It was difficult to accept the Canadian's story in its entirety, illogical to disbelieve it completely. Wherever the truth lay, there was one thing that was certain, Campbell was a badly shaken and frightened man. Raven glanced up at the mirror. The Crescent lay sleeping under a quilt of sunshine. He walked as far as the Fiat and bent down as though adjusting the thonged back of his sandal.

There *was* something fixed to the fuel tank. He fumbled under the car, tearing the object free of the sticky tape. When he straightened his back, he was holding a notebook about five inches by seven and bound in mottled cardboard. A quick look showed the finely drawn hieroglyphs that Campbell had mentioned. He locked the book in the glove compartment of the Pallas and walked into the cobbled mews. The small houses were gay with flowers and shrubs, the doors in bright colours. It was typical of Campbell to choose a Bramah lock to protect his home. The mechanism was virtually burglar-proof, the key almost impossible to reproduce from an impression.

Raven stepped into the narrow gold and white hallway and froze immediately. The house looked as if a hurricane had hit it. Someone had upturned a chest, littering the floor with hats, coats and magazines. There was more confusion in the sitting room on his left. Every possible hiding place had been searched. Drawers had been emptied, paintings removed from the walls, the carpet torn from its moorings. The state of the kitchen was even worse with sugar, tea, flour and salt emptied on to the floor. The table had been left upended.

He climbed the stairs, stepping over the mound of sheets and towels on the landing. The bed had been stripped, the wardrobe ransacked. Suits and shirts were thrown in every direction. Glass grated under Raven's feet and he bent down, picking up the silver picture-frame. The girl's picture had been taken against a background of magnificent redwood trees. She was presenting a three-quarter profile to the camera with her eyes almost closed and holding her shoulder length black hair behind her neck with one hand. Her wide artless grin showed that she wasn't taking herself seriously. Across the face of the picture were the words

Luv from Arbela

He shook the pieces of glass from the frame into the waste-paper basket and put the photograph back on the bedside table. He was aware of a slight touch of jealousy that a girl of such obvious looks and humour should throw in her lot with a rogue like Campbell. A likable rogue, but a rogue none the less.

The Canadians had given Raven his girlfriend's number. Raven lifted the phone and dialled. Nobody answered but Campbell had warned him that the other girl was out all day. Raven's second call was to New Scotland Yard.

'C 11. Extension 286.'

A familiar voice came on the line. 'Detective-Inspector Soo speaking.'

'I want you to meet me for lunch,' said Raven. 'It's important.'

'As long as it's no more Moroccan Chinese,' said Soo. 'I was in agony all night.'

Raven gave him the name of a riverside bar where they often ate.

'Get there as soon as you can.'

He put the phone down with a sense of security. It would have been no different if the rendezvous had been arranged for midnight in front of the Bolshoi Theatre. If Jerry said he'd be there, be there he would. The old magic never failed. Nobody kept a balance sheet. The help they afforded one another was sometimes barbed with criticism and this was either accepted or dismissed according to circumstance. Marriage had put Raven's sister at a distance so that in a sense Jerry was his family. There was certainly nobody closer to him.

He used the bathroom, staring out of the window on to the small patch of grass and solitary rosebush. A high brick wall surrounded the garden. There were no broken windows, no sign of a forcible entry anywhere. Whoever had been here had come in through the front door with a key as he had. The damage they'd done reminded him of the 'aggro-turnovers', specialities of the old school cops who used to descend on known villains, people who'd be unlikely to complain. There'd be no pretence at looking for incriminating evidence, no more than a blatant wrecking of property performed with supreme contempt. The difference in this case was that the visitors had known exactly what they were looking for.

There was no doubt left now in Raven's mind that Campbell was telling the truth. He went downstairs, stepping over the mess, and let himself out into the mews. He had gone ten yards when a woman's voice called after him.

'Good afternoon!'

He turned sharply, shielding his eyes as he looked up into the sunshine. The woman was leaning from a second floor window in the house next door, a woman in her late thirties with soft blonde hair tied back with a ribbon, and ample breasts.

'Hello,' he said uncertainly.

She glanced right and left and leaned a little further over the windowsill, inspecting him closer.

'You *are* from the police, aren't you?'

'That's right,' he replied.

'She wagged a hand frantically. 'Don't go away. I'll be right down.'

He moved to the cream coloured door. A small brass plate read

William Hertigant M.D.

The door opened from inside, offering a glimpse of oatmeal walls, a sheepskin rug and red roses.

'I guessed as much,' she said eagerly. Her face was slightly flushed and her breath smelled of scotch. She lowered her voice confidentially, a fellow upholder of law and order. 'My husband and I were talking to the other officer, the one who came last night. We always suspected there was something wrong, you know. I mean the way Mr Campbell behaved.'

He nodded without replying. She had a good throat and her arm movements made the most of it.

'Would you care to come in for a moment?'

He shook his head. 'You don't know the name of the other officer?'

He could see the bottles and decanter in the room at the end of the hallway.

'He didn't tell us,' she answered. 'We were just coming home as he was leaving. We guessed it was drugs of course. My husband's a doctor, you know. You could smell the marijuana when they'd smoke it in the garden. He and the girl. Nobody ever came to the house except her, and of course they're both Canadians.'

The curtains in Campbell's house were drawn. It was impossible for her to have seen the havoc inside. Raven smiled bleakly.

'I think you've got your facts all wrong, Mrs Hertigant. My advice to you is to keep that sort of gossip to yourself.'

Her face reddened and she closed the door quickly.

The Bean and Barley took its name from one of the soups on its menu. It was a bar-restaurant specializing in salt beef and pastrami, set between two paper warehouses on the south bank of the river near Vauxhall. A kosher sign was displayed on the window, but the waiters and chef were Spanish. The customers supported a mixed bag of religions. The place was popular with entertainers and sportsmen. Framed and autographed pictures of actors, jockeys and pugilists hung on the walls. The owner was an Australian and one-time conman known as Fatass Fred Feldman. Feldman ran a tight ship where his customers' money and liberty were considered sacrosanct. He gave generously to police charities, donated a case of scotch whisky to the local station at Christmas and mistrusted all cops in and out of uniform, apart from Raven.

The exception stemmed from the fact that a word of advice from Raven had saved the Australian from spending a number of summers and winters in jail on the Isle of Wight. Raven swung the Citroën on to a narrow strip of hardtop sealed by a padlocked chain. Beyond it was the river and the restaurant parking space. Raven gave the padlock the clout needed to unfasten it.

The big room and the bar were crowded, the atmosphere rich with cigar smoke and the smell of fried fish. Feldman rose from his usual place near the door, enormous buttocks spreading. He wrapped an arm around Raven's shoulders.

'How are you, me old mate! The Chinaman's in the Snug, waiting.' He jerked his head backwards, indicating the small annexe at the end of the restaurant. He had the easy manner and ready smile of his old occupation.

'See that we're left alone,' said Raven. 'We'll eat the usual. Meatballs, rice and coleslaw, a large Pernod and a cold bottle of beer.'

'It's on it's way,' said Feldman and waddled towards the kitchen.

Three steps led down to the alcove. There was just enough room for a table, two chairs and space for the waiter to move behind them. The low ceiling was buttressed with beams hewn from ships' timbers and the Thames was no more than six feet beneath the windows. There was a clear view of the Tate Gallery on the far side of the river.

Soo moved the bowl of freesias on the table, wearing the self-effacing smile that concealed the explosive power of a cheetah. He had on a grey mohair suit, button-down shirt and knitted silk tie. The waiter was on Raven's heels, carrying the drinks. Raven lifted the glass of beer.

'I have penetrated your disguise. You are none other than Jerry Soo, the Master Detective!'

Soo swirled the ice-cubes in his glass, his small

black eyes disappearing at the limits of his smile.

'We're gentlemen in C 11, not bums. And we have to dress the part. *Loch heim!*'

The food was placed on the table, hot and appetizing. 'We'll eat first, talk later,' said Raven.

Sunshine spread across the surface of the water below. Boys were fishing with homemade rods from the mudflats near the bridge. The moment the plates had been taken away, Raven pushed the small notebook across the table at Soo.

'Take a look at that,' he invited.

Soo turned the pages with slender fingers. His hands and feet were in contradiction to the rest of his body, fineboned and delicate. He closed the book on the hieroglyphics.

'I wouldn't be certain, but I'd say it's Korean. They used to use the Chinese symbols, but they've got their own script now.'

'Can you get it translated for me?' asked Raven.

Soo's face was mildly curious. 'I think so, yes.'

'How soon?'

'As soon as I learn to walk on water.'

'I'm serious,' urged Raven. 'Something's come up since I saw you last night.'

'You don't have to tell me,' said Soo. 'I can read the signals from here. One of your sordid acquaintances on temporary leave-of-absence from jail has conned you into some kind of foolishness. And the ex-Detective-Inspector's about to strike again.'

Raven ordered two more drinks. When the waiter had gone he leaned across the table behind a warning forefinger.

'It isn't a sordid acquaintance, Jerry. It's an

intelligent thief who's in fear of his life. We're dealing with dope smuggling in a big, big way.'

Soo's rounded mouth let out a low whistle. 'Dope smuggling no less.'

'That's right,' Raven insisted. 'And possibly worse.'

'That'll be enough to go on with,' said Soo. 'And that's why you want this stuff translated?'

'As soon as possible.'

Soo's expression told Raven that he had hit lucky. 'It just so happens that Louise has an uncle who speaks Korean,' said Soo. 'He lived in Seoul. I could try to get hold of him.'

'You could take the afternoon off,' said Raven.

Soo grinned. 'I'll tell my boss that you said so.'

Raven passed another sheet of paper across the table. 'There are two names there. Arbela Stewart and Roddy Campbell. Neither of them's got any form as far as I know, but there's bound to be something about Campbell. What I want to know is the following. Has Arbela Stewart been taken into custody anywhere in the Met within the last twenty-four hours? If so, I want the nature of the charge, the name of the arresting officer and the place she's being held.'

Soo used a toothpick to scratch his scalp. 'That shouldn't be difficult. How about Campbell?'

'Anything at all you can find. How soon can you do it, Jerry?'

Soo consulted an old-fashioned nickel watch. 'It depends on how soon I get hold of the uncle. He's eighty-two and lives way out in the East End. He might not be at home. When the weather's fine, he likes to sit in the park.'

Raven waved for the check. 'Is this going to run you into problems? How much attention will you be drawing to yourself?'

Soo shrugged, his grin wide. 'With a face like mine I'm *always* drawing attention to myself. There's no big sweat there. All that's involved is a signature. If I'm lucky, maybe not even that.'

'I'll tell you as much as I can when we meet,' said Raven. 'I have to move fast. What time do you think you can make it?'

Soo measured distance and time through half-closed eyes. 'You'd better come to my place at six o'clock. If I'm not back by then Louise will let you in.'

A quick feeling of doubt flared in Raven's mind. 'How about this uncle of hers, Jerry? I'm in trouble if any of this gets out. Can we trust him?'

'He's Chinese,' said Soo. 'And just in case you don't fully appreciate what that means, he'll have buried more secrets than you and I put together. O.K., six o'clock and don't forget to bring the flowers for Louise. You've really got her conned. She refers to you as "the perfect English gentleman". She should know you as well as I do.' He lifted a finger and disappeared.

Raven sat for five more minutes then started to make his way out. Feldman rose from his seat near the door and crooked a finger. Raven followed him into a room that had been turned into a facsimile of a cabin on a windjammer, down to the brass-framed porthole and spittoon. The door was cork-lined and soundproofed. The Australian lowered himself on to a horsehair sofa, coughing heavily. He clutched at his chest, looking up at Raven with swimming eyes.

'I'm getting old,' he said hoarsely.

Raven stayed standing. 'We all are. What have you lured me in here for?' He shook his head at the box of *Partagas*. Feldman rolled a cigar between thumb and forefinger, sniffed it and struck a match.

'A friend of mine saw a friend of yours the other day. He was calling himself by another name.'

'Who was?' said Raven. 'My friend or yours?'

'Yours.' The coughing started again and Feldman wiped his mouth on the back of his hand.

Raven moved back out of range. 'Careful, you're spraying. Is that all?'

'Don't be so bleedin' stand-offish,' said Feldman. He slid back the front of a cupboard, revealing a row of bottles. 'Have a liqueur or a glass of my vintage.'

'No, thanks,' said Raven. 'I'm in a hurry.'

'You always are.' Feldman slammed the cupboard shut again. He leaned back looking like a Jewish Buddha. 'That is to say *he* didn't call himself by this other name. Somebody else did. But it comes to the same. He was Mr Bates instead of Commander Drake.'

'Drake!' Raven's face betrayed all the distaste that the name evoked. Feldman was a source of information on many subjects, but he chose to be mysterious.

The Australian rose and reached for an ashtray. 'I thought you'd like to know.'

'Your friend was probably mistaken,' said Raven. 'Or Drake could have been acting on instructions.' Odd how the old official jargon tripped to the tongue. Drake might well have been on a job. Thieves weren't alone in using aliases. Plainclothesmen often employed them.

'No mistakes, mate!' Feldman shook his head, dislodging the ash on to his trousers. 'It was Drake all right. He was probably holding his hand out. The bastard's been on the take for years.'

Raven shrugged. 'You and I know that, but nobody's been able to prove it.'

'And you know why?' Spittle arched from Feldman's lips. 'They're all in it together, that's why. All the ones that matter. It's like you investigating me and me investigating you.'

'Not quite,' Raven said drily. 'You're crooked. I'm not.'

Feldman waved it aside. 'But you know what I mean. Look how many senior-ranking cops have been shoved inside this year, all of them attached to the Yard. Bribery, corruption. You name it, they did it. You don't think they're the only ones, do you?'

'You're preaching to the converted,' said Raven. 'But there's nothing I can do about it. Thanks for the tip, Fred. We'll be in touch.'

He drove to Chelsea and spent the next hour in the public library. A girl gave him a world almanac and Starke's *International Law*. He carried the two volumes to a desk near the window. The old man opposite was snoring gently beneath an injunction to silence. There was no need to take notes. What

Raven wanted was set out in clear terms on page 223 of Starke's book.

Diplomatic agents enjoy absolute immunity from the criminal jurisdiction of the receiving State and immunity from its civil and administrative jurisdiction. The person of a diplomatic agent is inviolable and he is not liable to any form of arrest or detention.

And further on

This immunity of diplomatic envoys extends not merely to their own persons but to their suite and members of their family forming part of their household provided that they are not nationals of the receiving State.

He picked up the second book. The information here was contained in yet another single paragraph. North Korea, the Democratic Peoples Republic of North Korea, had a Soviet-type constitution that was suposed to be based on that of Bulgaria. Created in 1948, its recognition by the Russian bloc was immediate. The Western powers delayed theirs until much later. That of the United Kingdom was finally accorded in 1976.

The staff of the London embassy was listed as: Ambassador Extraordinary and Plenipotentiary: His Excellency Won Chang (1977). First Secretary: Nam Cho. Second Secretary: Duk Kwon. Attaché (Cultural and Press): In Soo Pai.

There were a couple of lines about the lopsided trade balance between North Korea and the U.K., and a piece that dealt with the country's six hundred years of independence before its integration into the Japanese Empire when it became known as Choson or 'morning calm'.

He returned the books to the desk, drove south to the Embankment and parked in the alleyway next to the Herborium. There was nobody in the store. The sunblinds were at half-mast in front of a motley display of herbs, ginseng, bamboo knick-knacks and remaindered volumes of poetry. A large lizard sitting in a marble mortar watched Raven with unwinking eyes.

He crossed the road and climbed down the steps to the gangway. As he stepped on deck he heard his name being called from the neighbouring boat. He looked across the ten feet of water. Saul Belasus was lying in the sunshine clad in a pair of boxer shorts, his head resting on the Great Dane's flank. He flapped an arm vaguely.

'Ringadingding, man! Your phone.'

He closed his eyes again. Raven let himself into his sitting room. The phone would really have had to be ringing to make an impression on his neighbour. Belasus was a chemistry graduate who'd worked ten years for a major drug house, living on canned food and sleeping on a camp bed. At thirty-two, he'd thrown up his job, brought his savings to England and bought the Herborium and river-boat. He mended broken wings for birds and minded his own business.

There were clean sheets and towels in the linen cupboard. Raven made up the big bed in the guest room, a replica of his own down to the cedarwood wardrobe and separated from it by the bathroom.

His next stop was on the corner of Fulham Road and Callow Street. The girl selling flowers there offered a smile and unfailing good humour summer and winter alike. She gave him the roses he asked for, choosing the blooms with care.

'You don't buy as many flowers as you used to,' she said, chiding him. 'Unless you're getting them somewhere else.'

'No one to give them to,' he said, smiling.

She gave him change for the five pound note. 'Poor fellow! I'd take you on myself if I wasn't married.'

The yellow roses smelled of country gardens. 'I've got a feeling you'd be sorry,' he answered.

He reached Rotherhithe just before six o'clock. The highrise building where Jerry Soo lived towered over the coal and timber wharves. It was a middle-income investment project and properly supervised. There was no vandalism and the lifts worked. He went as far as the top floor. The picture window at the end of the corridor presented a distant view of Greenwich, the river between winding back on itself like a snake. He pressed the buzzer and the door opened immediately.

Louise Wang was a good six inches taller than Soo, with long legs displayed in Shantung trousers. Her straight black hair hung in a shining sheet to her shoulders and was cut with a fringe. He handed her the bunch of yellow roses. She smiled, thanking him in accentless English.

'They're in the sitting room.'

He followed her into a long room with french windows opening on to a balcony. They had lived there for three years. Louise had supervised the decorations and supplied some of the furniture. She'd created an impression of light and space that somehow managed to survive the drabness of winter, The walls were cream, there were bamboo chairs and couches and a lot of traditional Chinese bric-à-brac. Soo's Abyssinian cat lay coiled on the low opium table. Near it were an ivory mah jong set and Soo's stamp collection. Greenery trailed from two large porcelain jars that had come from Taiwan.

Soo was standing in front of one of the open french windows, still elegant in grey flannel. Seated beside him in a shaft of sunlight was an old man dressed in a high-necked tunic suit and wearing felt slippers. Wispy grey hair straggled over his face down to his chin where it hung in a scanty goat's beard. His skin was the colour and texture of beeswax, his hands like birds' claws with very long nails. He looked up blearily at Raven.

Louise touched her uncle's cheek with tender fingers. 'I have to go to rehearsal. Will you be here when I come back, John? Can't you stay for supper?'

'I would if I could,' he said. 'But there's too much to do. Thanks all the same.'

She embraced them in turn, her uncle last. She turned to Soo.

'You'll see that he gets home safely?'

'Of course,' Soo nodded, touching the old man's shoulder. Raven had seen it before in Hong Kong, the affection and veneration afforded the elderly. Soo waited till he heard the elevator on its downward journey then spoke in rapid Cantonese. The old man's smile disclosed yellow teeth pegged into receding gums.

'He says to talk English,' Soo explained.

A bony hand grasped Raven's. 'He wanted to see you himself,' went on Soo. 'He'll tell you why later. How about a drink?'

'Later,' said Raven. Louise's excuse for leaving had been contrived, he was certain of it. Something in Soo's manner, Louise's absence, the fact that her uncle was present, all added to his sense of expectancy. 'O.K.,' he said. 'What did you get?'

Soo unzipped a briefcase and handed a sheet of paper to Raven. It was a photocopy of a Criminal Records file headed C 11/4961/74. The number identified it as being the 4961st file opened in 1974.

Known Active but unconvicted in the United Kingdom. Roderic Ian Campbell born 11/8/41 New Westminster, British Columbia Canada. Subject educated St Dominic's School Vancouver and Schloss Mayenfels Baselland Switzerland. Subject first came to attention of police when arrested in Stratford Ontario, 20/1/1970 together with Paul Stewart (q.v.) and charged with theft of postage stamps valued at $87,000. Charges dismissed due to failure of prosecuting witnesses to attend court proceedings. Subject next arrested in Vancouver City, British Columbia, 4/9/1972 together with Paul Stewart and interrogated concerning theft of twenty platinum bars valued $210,000 from Jeweller's Exchange Building. Subject released 7/9/1972, insufficient evidence to warrant prosecution. Subject is only son of Ian Campbell J.P. of Vancouver, founder and owner of New Westminster Lumber Company.

Subject believed to have left Canada some time in 1973 in company of Paul Stewart's widow Arbela Stewart. Subject suspected of being responsible numerous thefts and burglaries involving jewellery while in the U.K. Subject speaks fluent French and German and is known to travel extensively. Attached photograph of subject taken at Sandown Park racecourse March 1975. Subject's present address and whereabouts unknown.

'There are four more pages in the original,' said Soo. 'And you're mentioned in dispatches. You know, the times you interrogated him and all that. The rest of it's irrelevant. I tried to get a copy of the photograph, but it came out looking like something out of the *Psychic News*.'

'I don't need it,' said Raven. 'How about the girl?'

Soo filled a translucent bowl with rice wine and gave it to the old man who took it in both hands and sipped greedily.

'No one of that name has been arrested or charged during the past forty-eight hours,' said Soo. 'Not in the Metropolitan Police area.'

The only sound in the room was that of the old man slurping. Soo reached into the briefcase again and came out holding the small notebook that Raven had given him. There were some pieces of paper tucked under the cover. The writing on them was shaky. The translation dealt with dates, sums of money and a list of Asian names.

Raven glanced up. 'That's all?' He knew the way Soo's mind worked. Something was being held back.

Soo shrugged. 'You'd better get yourself a drink.

Raven crossed the room to the cabinet and poured himself a scotch and water. Adrenalin surged into his bloodstream for a second time that day, honing his brain and nervous system.

'O.K. Let's have it.'

'There are two Western names in that book,' said Soo. 'Underwood and Drake.'

Raven swallowed the drink without tasting it. 'Go on.'

'There are entries totalling $110,000 against each name, John.'

Raven took his empty glass to the balcony. His hand shaking and out of control.

'Who's Underwood?'

'There are five of them on the establishment. Five Underwoods and six Drakes. Detective-Inspector Glen Underwood works out of the Drug Squad. He's a man who's obviously going places. He joined in '60, moved over to plainclothes in '62. Promoted detective-sergeant in '65 and joined the gangbusters in '74.'

Raven turned. His hands were no longer shaking. 'I don't remember any Underwood.'

'You wouldn't,' said Soo. 'He took your place when you quit. He was Drake's right-hand man for a while then both of them moved. Drake got his halo and Underwood went to the Drug Squad. He's got a beautiful record, John. The Queen's Medal for bravery and no less than five commendations. Guess who sat on his Promotion Board, the one that upped him to the Drug Squad.'

'I don't believe it.' Raven's voice was so quiet it

could hardly be heard. 'I don't believe it,' he said much louder. 'Do you realize what this means to me, Jerry?'

Soo's burly shoulders rose and fell. 'I don't know a thing. I'm waiting for you to tell me.'

Raven closed the french windows, sneaking a sideways look at the old Chinese.

'You don't have to worry about him,' said Soo and sank in a cushioned bamboo chair. 'Enchant us with the magic of your storytelling.'

It took Raven the best part of half an hour, editing nothing.

Soo voiced the expected objection immediately. 'I believe every word of it, John. Which is why you're going to lay the whole package on the Commissioner's desk. Let *him* work it out with the Foreign Office. You go off at half-cock as you usually do and the odds are on you getting your head blown off. Or maybe you don't think this is possible?'

'Anything's possible,' said Raven. 'I could get killed crossing the street.'

The two men challenged one another across the room, the old man sipping his rice wine between them.

'What are you trying to sell me, Jerry?' Raven said finally. 'This is *Drake* for God's sake. Don't you understand that I'd have given an arm for a chance like this? And now I've got it, you want me to turn it over to someone else?'

Soo shook his head sadly. 'The man's an obsession with you.'

Raven pounced on the word, reddening under his suntan. 'You're fucking well right the man's an obsession! Is that so surprising? He haunted me for ten years, Jerry, doing his best to scupper me!'

'You could have soldiered on,' said Soo. 'You didn't really want to stay.'

There was a lump in Raven's throat that he couldn't dislodge. It was hard to keep his voice down.

'Try your half-assed theories on somebody else, Jerry. I don't buy them.'

'Of course not.' Soo was smiling but his tone was level. 'You don't like facing facts. You never have done. Take this present business for instance. It isn't Campbell who matters or the fact that this girl's life might be in danger. The fact that foreign diplomats are running dope into the country doesn't matter either. What's important is your vendetta with Drake. And now you think you've got him in your sights, you don't want anyone else near the trigger.'

Raven wet his lips, mouth dry. The first drink had been wasted. He poured himself a second.

'I've got to do this my own way, Jerry. And I expect you to understand.'

'I understand.' Soo's laugh rang like a gong. 'You always do things your own way. That's what worries me.'

Raven's face and voice were obstinate. 'Retribution, Jerry. That's what it is. And I'm wielding the hammer.'

Soo blinked, his gesture one of defeat. He spoke in Cantonese. The old man's voice was like a whisper at the end of a tunnel.

'These people very bad. Too strong. Red Dragon

Society. Kill many. North Korea, all over. Snake grow horns and turn into dragon. Very dangerous.'

He drew his forefinger across the front of his throat. Soo spoke again in Chinese and turned to Raven.

'I just told him that he's wasting his time. You fancy yourself as a hero.'

'I'm a hunter not a hero,' said Raven. 'And hunt is what I'm about to do. If you're a friend of mine you'll help me.'

A tug hooted upstream. The old man's eyes were closed, his face at peace in the sunshine.

'You win,' said Soo. 'You generally do. What evidence have you got to go on?'

'Enough to make you want me to stick it in front of the Commissioner,' said Raven. 'A man's been shot at, his house ransacked, his girlfriend abducted. And the book that's the cause of it all has Drake's name in it and the name of a man on the Drug Squad. Don't talk to me about evidence. In any case I don't *need* any evidence for what I'm going to do.'

'Don't tell me!' said Soo, holding up a hand. 'I'd rather not hear.'

'Do you know where Underwood lives?' asked Raven.

'I read his file,' said Soo. 'I even know his blood type. He's single and lives at 32 Palliser Close, Wimbledon Common. Don't come to me for bail if you're busted.'

'We're the *good* guys,' said Raven. 'Can't you accept that?'

'Tell it to the hatchetman when he comes at you

swinging,' said Soo. 'Am I to assume that you're determined not to let me do anything about all this?'

It was after seven and he had to meet Campbell by eight. The days of explanations and excuses were over between Soo and him.

'Nothing at all,' said Raven. 'Not yet at least. I promised I wouldn't blow the whistle.'

'You promised.' Soo shook his head. 'You're too old to be a Boy Scout.'

'I always was,' said Raven.

Soo came as far as the lift with him. 'Take care, John. And because of Drake take special care.'

ARBELA STEWART

July 20

She woke disturbed by the light that was piercing
the curtains. She could see the wallpaper now,
patterned with red, blue and yellow flowers. She was
lying in a four-poster bed under a low, bulging
ceiling. There were rugs on the polished uneven
floor, a wardrobe and a dressing-table with winged
mirrors near the window. There were no sheets on
the bed, but the blankets were clean. Her dress,
sandals and underclothes were on the floor near the
bed. She remembered going to sleep in her clothes
then waking during the night and throwing them
off. She'd been allowed to keep her things after
they'd searched her, but her watch had stopped.
She lowered herself to the boards, the cheval-mirror
reflecting her long-legged naked body. She pulled
the curtain back cautiously, letting in still more
light. A screen of heavy-duty wire had been screwed
to the outside of the window frame. There was saw-
dust on the ledge and the scars in the wood were
fresh. The room was above the kitchen. They'd
brought her in the back way and she recollected the
grey plastic dustbins and the arch at the end of the
brick-paved courtyard. Through it she could see
loose boxes now unused. There was an open garage,
the Mercedes limousine inside. Beyond the outbuildings there were trees in every direction, a
forest of firs, pine and beeches, solid green in the
early morning sunlight. More screws inserted

through the sashes prevented them from being lowered or raised.

A hand basin was attached to the wall. There was soap and a towel. She turned on the hot tap. It was some time before the water arrived, rusty in colour, the pipes that carried it clanking and groaning. She washed and cleaned her teeth as best she could with her fingers. There was a spray bottle of *Paco Rabanne* in her bag and some tissues. The package of Macdonald Export held nine cigarettes, but she had no matches. She put on her clothes and folded the blankets neatly. Then she wound her watch and set the hands at eight o'clock. It was no more than a guess but at least it linked her with passing time.

The door was locked and the key had been removed. She peeped through the keyhole, but the field of vision was narrow. All she could see was the wall and the top of the staircase. People were moving about below and she could smell coffee burning. She went through the wardrobe and dressing table, finding no more than some lavender bags and a clock key. There was nothing she could use in an attempt to escape. She climbed on to the four-poster and shut her eyes. It was incredible, looking back, that she could have made such a fool of herself the night before. All she had to do was pick up the phone and dial 999. Her problem had been a guilty conscience. Part of her brain had been expecting disaster ever since Roddy had told her what he planned to do. The arrival of a detective had seemed no more than the logical sequence. Even now she couldn't make up her mind whether or not he was a genuine cop.

At the beginning he had seemed the epitome of what she expected a British detective to be like. Once in the car, he'd told her that Roddy had been arrested and was being held at Harrow Road police station. She'd believed him completely, her only concern for her lover. The first hint that something was wrong had come when instead of taking a left turn at Marble Arch, the detective had driven straight down into the vast Park Lane subterranean garage. He'd stopped at the foot of the ramp with an excuse about needing petrol, but for petrol he didn't have to have a parking voucher. The entrance was unmanned and there was no one behind. As he reached out to take a voucher from the vending machine she'd managed to get a door open. But he was on her before she could go any further, jolting her head with the force of his slaps, his mask dropped.

'Another move like that,' he snarled, 'and I'll scar you for life!'

There was nothing in front of them but lines of parked cars, all of them empty. He seemed to know exactly where he was going, wheeling through the cars and stopping beside a Mercedes. She recognized the embassy limousine immediately. The blinds were down in the rear windows. The detective reached across her, the smell of his body rank.

'In the other car,' he ordered.

Hands grabbed her as she moved forward. After the first instinctive struggle she put up no more resistance and lay limp on the back seat. She could see the lighted office at the foot of an exit ramp a couple of hundred yards away. Crouching in front of her was one of the guards from the embassy. The Korean chauffeur was at the wheel, Nam Cho sitting beside him. The guard pulled her face forward on to the gauze pad he was holding. She thrashed about uselessly, breathing in the sweet sickly fumes. There was a dim memory of voices as the car passed through the exit, a dreamlike vision of lighted buses floating in air, a corridor down which she flew into darkness. When she came to her senses again, the car was deep in country lanes, the road unreeling in the glare of the headlamps. Hedges and telephone posts rushed by on both sides. Nam Cho and the driver were still in front, the security guard next to her, but the detective had gone. She closed her eyes quickly but not quickly enough. The guard covered her head with a rug that smelled of dogs.

She remembered the feeling of claustrophobia, the pressure of the guard's hands as she clawed desperately in search of air. There was a filthy taste in her mouth, a jackhammer at work in her head. The car slowed. She heard gates being opened, the rumble of tyres crossing a cattle-grid then they stopped. The rug was removed from her head and she climbed out of the limousine. The deep bubbling song of a nightingale came from the woods behind them. They entered the house through a vast old-fashioned kitchen bright with whitewash and copper pans. The guard searched her in front of the others, his hands rough and intimate. Her watch had been working then. It was ten o'clock. There were stags' heads in the timbered hallway, the hair moth-eaten, glassy eyes staring at pictures of bygone cricket teams, dead flies and leaded windows. The air in the place was stuffy as though the house had long been closed and only just reopened. The guard bustled her upstairs into a room and turned the key on her. From the moment they'd pulled her into the limousine, no one had spoken a word to her. It was this silence that terrified her more than anything else.

Now she opened her eyes, hearing the creak of someone coming up the stairs. The door opened. The guard was dressed in his factory blues and felt-soled slippers, his newly shaven scalp shining. He crooked a finger at her to follow. Daylight made the house and furnishings even shabbier. There was dust everywhere and the stair-carpet was worn. It was ten past eight by the grandfather clock at the foot of the stairs. The front door was still heavily bolted. The guard pushed her into a room where Nam Cho was waiting. He was wearing charcoal grey slacks and a silk polo-necked sweater. The table was laid with breakfast for two. Coffee, toast, boiled eggs and marmalade. One of the eggs had already been eaten. Through the windows behind Nam Cho a driveway cut through an unkempt lawn and vanished into the trees. The scene was serene in the sunlight. Nam Cho wiped his mouth with his napkin and waved invitation.

'Sit down, Mrs Stewart.'

He poured a second cup of coffee for her and pushed the toast rack in her direction. Hunger gave her the courage to eat. She cracked open the second boiled egg. He watched her as she buttered the toast, his voice full of its customary courtesy.

'Do you value your life, Mrs Stewart?'

'Everyone values their life.' Her voice sounded

false as though she was reading lines in a play. She forced herself to swallow. Each mouthful gave her strength.

'Very good!' Nam Cho smiled like a teacher encouraging a promising pupil. 'Now we come to the second part of the question. Do you value the life of your lover?'

There were bookcases filled with giltbound volumes and the date 1735 was carved over the stone fireplace. She felt a million miles from home with stars colliding around her.

'The police will be looking for me by now.' She tried to say it with confidence but failed.

'Wrong,' he said behind wagging forefinger. 'You sent your flatmate a telegram from Edinburgh last night explaining that you'd gone there with Mr Campbell. You assured her that you were perfectly safe and that there was no cause for her to worry. You'll send her more news later.'

She drank the coffee gratefully. It was fresh and strong, recharging her body and brain with energy. She lighted a cigarette, using the matches that were on the table. She kept the box near her.

'Why are you doing this to me? What is it you want?' More lines from yet another play.

He put both elbows on the table and rested his chin in his palms.

'Who sent you to the embassy?'

'The agency.'

'And all you had in mind was a temporary job for six weeks?'

'That's right.'

He took his chin from his hands and shook his

head slowly. 'You're a psychopathic liar but it makes no difference. Why did you sneak back into the embassy that day? I'm sure you remember the occasion.'

She moved nervously. 'It was pure chance. I'd no idea . . .' she broke off lamely.

'That there was money in the safe?' His smile was broad. 'Come on now, Mrs Stewart. That was why you came to us in the first place, wasn't it? You'd been told about the safe. What I want to know is *who* told you.'

'What we did was wrong,' she said quietly. 'And I'm sorry.'

He moved quickly, taking her wrist in his grasp. He tightened his hold till her arm stiffened in agony. Pain invaded her neck and head and she was unable to move.

'A wolf with his fangs in the throat of a sheep is neither right nor wrong. You're a fool and you live in a fool's world. I'm not interested in your views on morality.'

He released her wrist as suddenly as he had taken it. She kneaded the numbed flesh tenderly.

'We'll do whatever it is that you want,' she pleaded.

He smiled again as though nothing had happened between them. 'Let me explain something to you, Mrs Stewart. Something that will help you to understand my position and your own. If that book isn't returned within the next forty-eight hours, the entire embassy staff will be recalled to Pyong Yang. Failure has no defence in my country. There will be no trial. Do I make myself clear?'

She nodded quickly, too scared to tell him that she'd no idea what he was talking about. Nam Cho was still smiling but his eyes were implacable.

'It's a simple equation. You and your lover expected money. You didn't find it. You found something else instead. Something I want. We've got to get hold of Campbell. Time's running out.'

It was the first indication that Roddy was free and she suddenly felt much better.

'I don't know where he is.' she said.

'You'd better think,' he answered. 'Unless the book is returned I shall kill you myself.'

She lighted another cigarette, her fingers shaking violently. She hated him seeing the effect he had on her but there was nothing that she could do about it.

'I don't *know* where he'd go,' she said desperately. 'I can only guess where he is if he's not in his house. His family is in Canada and he has no friends in this country. You've got to understand the way Roddy's mind works. He's a loner.'

Nam Cho nodded. 'You think he's out there somewhere looking for you?'

She thought of Roddy hunted, on the run yet knowing that she was in danger.

'He'll be looking for me!' This time she spoke with certainty.

'That's what I think,' said Nam Cho. 'If he gets in touch with the embassy the call will come here. When that happens I want your co-operation.'

She made a small gesture of defeat. 'You've got to believe me, Mr Nam Cho. I know nothing about a book, nothing about whatever it is that he's taken.

But I promise you this. We don't want money, we don't want anything. All we need is the chance to go.'

He seemed to look through her eyes and into her head. 'It's too late for games, Mrs Stewart.'

'Whatever you want me to do, I'll do,' she promised.

He clapped his hands sharply. The security guard accompanied her back upstairs and turned the key on her. She counted the matches she had taken. There were six cigarettes and eleven matches.

GLEN UNDERWOOD

July 20

It was cool in the bank vault after the heat of the street. He closed the empty box and handed the second key to the guard who made an entry in the book in front of him and looked up smiling.

'Lovely day again, Mr O'Dwyer. Not that you see too much of it sitting down here.'

'Lovely,' said Underwood and went upstairs, the briefcase tucked firmly under his arm. Instinct told him that it was time for the contents of his safe deposit box to be under his control. He drove home to Wimbledon Common, hid the briefcase under his bed and called his office. Sergeant Tanner was at his desk.

'I've just left the dentist,' said Underwood. 'I'm on my way back now.'

It was three o'clock when he made his way up the ramp leading from the police garage to the main entrance of New Scotland Yard. There were the usual lines in front of the reception desks. The benches where a complainant had his first interview were crowded. Subsequent inquiries might take him past the security guards to an office of any one of the eight floors but this was where it all started. Beyond the door on the right was a row of interrogation rooms, bugged and fitted with secret spyholes. Underwood was wearing an alpaca jacket and a tie with his shirt. He flashed his warrant card at the security guards and stepped into the lift.

The fourth floor was given over to C13 which

consisted of five squads. Forgery, Illegal Immigration, Arts and Antiques, Post Office Frauds and the Drug Squad.

He walked the hundred yards along the corridor to his office, exchanging greetings with familiar faces. He opened the door, wincing as his nose met the acrid stink of tobacco smoke. Underwood's desk faced the window, Sergeant Tanner's was at right angles to it. Tanner had the phone clamped between shoulder and cheek and looked up, showing a thumb. Half a dozen cigarettes, all of them lighted, were smouldering in two ashtrays in front of him.

Underwood touched a switch and the air-conditioning system whined into action, dragging fresh oxygen into the room.

'Why do you have to stink the place out?' asked Underwood, looking at Tanner with distaste. The Sergeant was wearing the same clothes as on the previous day down to the palm-patterned shirt. Underwood poked through the papers on his desk, wondering how to break the news to Drake. There'd been no word from the Koreans since he'd delivered Arbela Stewart to the Park Lane garage. He'd gone home and considered his next move. Nam Cho had forced him into an error of judgement. If he'd had time to reflect, he wouldn't have made the false arrest. He'd had to show his face on two occasions and it left him exposed. There was the girl who shared the apartment with Stewart. He'd talked to her for twenty minutes. Arbela Stewart could wreck him on an abduction charge alone, given the testimony of her flatmate and the woman in the mews. One way or another it was Arbela Stewart who had to be dealt with. He was fighting for his life and shouldering too much weight on his own. There'd been no mention of Drake, no suggestion that he should be brought in to help. Yet it was Drake who'd set the whole thing up, stage-managing the Promotion Board and arranging the transfer to the Drug Squad. Drake had covered his tracks well. His only contact with the North Koreans was the envelope that Underwood left in the Bowls Club foot-locker once a month. But he had to be shown that he couldn't just walk away when the action got heavy.

Tanner came off the line, choosing one of the cigarettes still burning in front of him.

'That was Caroline Brewster's mouthpiece. Patrick O'Callaghan.'

'What does he want?' Underwood kept Tanner on for two reasons, his stupidity and his ambition.

Tanner's nicotine-stained teeth badly needed attention. 'They want the witnesses to attend. They're pleading Not Guilty.'

Underwood scribbled his initials on a couple of forms. 'So?'

'Stoned out of her mind with four ounces of hash in her handbag! *Not Guilty?*'

'Did you get a statement?' asked Underwood.

Tanner shook his head. 'Only her name and address. She knew the form.'

'Then she couldn't have been that far gone.' Underwood came to his feet. 'You've got a mouth like a barn door in a high wind and O'Callaghan will run rings round you if you're not careful. Check your notebook. That's the first thing he'll ask to see. And make sure you can read your own writing.'

He rinsed his mouth in the lavatory and tied a better knot in his tie. Once beyond the pass door, the passages were carpeted and the offices sound-proofed. He knocked and put his head into a room where a girl with a fringe was hammering on a typewriter.

'Detective-Inspector Underwood. Is there any chance of seeing Commander Drake?'

She suspended her typing, looking back over her shoulder. 'He went down to the canteen. He won't be back this afternoon. He's got an appointment outside.'

He thanked her and went down again. The big canteen was crowded with men and women both in plain clothes and uniform. Underwood took his place in the line, trying to locate the man he was looking for as he shuffled forward. He was paying for his coffee when he saw Drake sitting alone at a table near the wall.

Underwood carried his cup across. 'Something's come up. I have to see you.'

Drake's steel-grey head lifted slowly. His heavy body was covered with shiny blue serge, his tie spotted with grease. A fixed smile was pasted on to his red face, but his eyes were mean.

'You'd better have a good reason for this,' he growled.

Underwood brushed the breadcrumbs from the other chair and sat down.

'There's trouble. I'm not carrying the can on my own. You've got to help me out.'

Drake folded his newspaper carefully, holding the

smile for the benefit of anyone who might have been looking.

'Keep your bloody voice down and try to look as if you're saying something pleasant.'

Underwood leaned across the table. 'A Canadian broke into the embassy yesterday. There was a shipment in the safe and he saw it. Nam Cho says . . .'

'Hold it!' Drake's head was erect like a snake about to strike. 'I don't *know* any bleedin' Nam Cho, got it? I never even heard of him. I warned you at the start. Any trouble, I said, and you're on your own and I meant it. You want my advice you'll put your skates on. There is just one more thing. Come near me again or as much as call me and you're for the breaker's yard.'

He jammed the newspaper in his sagging pocket and rolled away ponderously.

Fear and disbelief left Underwood staring into his coffee cup. A man eased himself into the seat Drake had just left.

'Congratulations!'

Underwood glanced up stonily. The newcomer was a canteen acquaintance who worked in the Personnel department of C5. The division that handled C.I.D. affairs, administration and operations, discipline and promotion.

'What are you talking about?' said Underwood.

The man sipped his coffee and made a face. 'Don't be coy,' he said, winking.

'I don't know what the fuck you're talking about,' Underwood said distinctly.

The other man's face lost its confidence. 'Promotion, isn't it? I mean, somebody pulls your file this morning and here you are with Drake. *And* he's on the Promotion Board again this month.'

It required an effort for Underwood to make his voice sound normal.

'*Who* pulled my file?'

The man shrugged. 'Jerry Soo. That Chinese cop who sometimes does Promotion Board research.'

'Never heard of him,' said Underwood.

'He's on the Judo team – or used to be,' the man enlarged. 'He was always with Raven, you remember, the guy who resigned after all that publicity on television a few years ago. Something to do with a Pole called Zaleski. You must remember Raven, for crissakes. You took his place in the Gangbusters Squad!'

Underwood nodded. His breathing was shallow and he could feel his heart banging. He managed a sort of smile.

'Well, if they make me Commissioner I'll buy you a box of cigars.'

He raised two fingers in farewell and walked blindly out of the building. He found himself on an empty bench where across the stretch of grass an old woman with cherries in her hat was feeding bread to the birds. He watched her, unseeing, trying to get his brain working again. What worried him was the business of somebody pulling his file. The name Jerry Soo still meant nothing but Raven rang a bell. It was something to do with Drake. Something that Drake had once said. After half an hour he returned to New Scotland Yard carrying a growing anxiety with him.

His next stop was C4, the Criminal Record Office.

A staff of over five hundred was employed, a hundred of these police officers, the rest civilians. Three million records were stored in the Department, half of them dormant and kept on microfilm. The files were kept up to date by the Registry. The Criminal Index was split into sections. *Nominal* listed the names of convicted persons and their aliases. *Method* dealt with the type of crime and m.o. used. Then there were the *Wanted* and *Cheque* indexes. In addition to these C4 housed the *Rogues Gallery* with more than a thousand photograph albums of known offenders.

Underwood filled in a form and waited his turn in the line that had formed near the counter. The clerk was in his shirt-sleeves, his red face and manner evidence that the heat was beginning to get to him. He grabbed Underwood's form, scanned it mechanically and did a double take.

'Jesus Christ!' he burst out. 'You'd think you people would be able to get it together!' He looked at the form again, this time more closely and apologized. 'Sorry, mate. I thought you were from C5. Only this'll be the second time this afternoon I've been asked to run this geezer through the machine. I can tell you this for nothing. *We've* got nothing on him. Who is he, anyway?'

Underwood shrugged. 'A villain.'

'Hang about,' said the clerk and walked away.

The man standing next on the line shook his head at Underwood. 'It's like asking them to part with their balls!'

The clerk was back, still holding Underwood's piece of paper. 'Try C11. O.K.?'

C11 was Criminal Intelligence and linked to Interpol. Though it indexed thousands of names of major criminals only a small percentage of them had records. Underwood made the trip downstairs, filled in yet another form and carried the folder he was given to a standup desk at the end of the room. The file contained all known details of Campbell's personal habits and characteristics, his associates and a record of the interrogations he had been subjected to. It took Underwood six minutes to find the lead he was looking for. It was an account of a burglary that had been committed three and a half years earlier in a block of flats off Belgrave Square. Campbell had been detained on the premises, submitted to a body-search with negative results and subsequently released.

The name of the senior investigating officer was given as John Raven, attached to New Scotland Yard, Serious Crimes Squad. Underwood signed the file across the counter and left, his palms sweating and the hand of fear cold on his back. He'd just remembered what and how he had heard about Raven. Drake had said it the day Underwood had joined the Gangbusters Squad.

This mob sticks together, get it? We do what we're told and we don't ask questions. You'll hear the name Raven, remember it! You're taking the bastard's place.

The warning had meant nothing then except that there was bad feeling between Drake and Raven. The trail led from Campbell to Raven to Soo. They were too close for comfort. Apart from Drake there were only two people who might have guessed or suspected what was going on. The first was Underwood's D.D.S., Barney Jessel. The Divisional Detective Superintendent was responsible for all-over strategy in the Drug Squad, but he had three areas to worry about and left Underwood strictly alone. Underwood had made the West End his own territory and with Tanner had run up a record of convictions that had impressed the Commissioner himself. Jessel was more than content. The only other person who might have caught on would have been Tanner, which was ridiculous. Tanner was a trained dog with a loud bark and no nose.

Soo's action remained an enigma, but the warning was clear. It was time to move and move fast. Underwood opened his office door. Tanner's electric teamaker was plugged in.

'Any calls?' asked Underwood. He wanted to be out of the building. Each phone call represented danger.

'Nothing,' said Tanner. He scratched the back of his neck with his thumb. 'You look rough. Is the tooth still bothering you?'

'It's the whole side of my head.' said Underwood. 'I'm taking tomorrow off. Don't forget you've got the Brewster girl in the morning. Bow Street, Court Number Two, eleven o'clock.'

He opened and closed his desk drawers casually. There was nothing there that could put them on his trail. He lifted the phone and called his superior.

'What's your problem?' asked Jessel who affected a no-nonsense manner in his telephone conversations.

Jessel was mobile. Underwood could hear the traffic noises in the background.

'The dentist just about murdered me this morning, sir. I'd like to take tomorrow off.'

There was no hint of suspicion in Jessel's voice. 'You want to be like me, Glen. Put 'em in a glass at night. What have you got for tomorrow?'

'A "Possession" case at Bow Street, that's all. Sergeant Tanner can deal with it.' He grinned across at his colleague who was dropping teabags into a stained metal pot.

'Then take the day,' said Jessel. 'And remember my advice. Have 'em all out!'

Underwood tidied the papers on his desk. 'I'm off, Tanner. And watch that O'Callaghan tomorrow!'

He checked out of the building and walked down the ramp to his car. The vehicle had been standing in the sun all the morning and the interior was stuffy. He wound down the windows. The radio sets were still operating. He'd no intention of going off the air. He didn't want to talk, but he certainly wanted to listen. His first stop was the British Airways office in Lower Regent Street. He bought himself a ticket from London to Paris for the following morning. He walked up the street to Air Canada and bought a seat on the plane from Paris to Montreal. There were fifty minutes at Charles de Gaulle for him to clear customs and immigration and check back in on the Air Canada flight. With the two tickets in his pocket he felt a lot safer. At the back of his mind, he'd always known that the run would have to end. It had been shorter than he'd hoped for, but he wasn't leaving empty-handed. What he had to do now was remove one of the links that connected him to the Koreans, Arbela Stewart.

He drove back to Wimbledon Common. It was after six and the people next door were already home. He put the aeroplane tickets with the money in the briefcase under the bed and turned on the bath. He made himself coffee and a sandwich while the water was running. He lay in the bath, running his plan through his head. The elements of success were there. Everything depended on how he combined them.

He towelled himself dry and dressed in a lightweight suit. He used dye and a piece of cotton to darken the circle of white in his hair. The snub-nosed Police Special in the bottom drawer of his desk had been given to him by a visiting Federal Narcotic Agent. He slipped it into his jacket pocket, sat on the bed and called the North Korean Embassy. An operator's voice interrupted the dialling tone.

'All calls to this number are being referred to Hartfield three eight four six.'

Underwood re-dialled and recognized Nam Cho's voice. 'Good news,' said Underwood. 'Can you get hold of twenty thousand within the next couple of hours? Used five and tens.'

Nam Cho's voice was pitched a little higher than usual. 'Where are you speaking from?'

'London. I can't talk over the phone, but the deal's on. The deal you asked for. The money's part of it.'

There was a pause before Nam Cho answered. 'You'd better come here.'

Underwood scribbled the directions on the pad

by the phone. 'I'll be there between nine and ten.'

He tore the sheet of paper from the scribbling-pad and checked the address in the A.A. guide. The village was on the edge of Ashdown Forest with the A22 the most direct route. But first he had another visit to make. He closed his front door gently and tiptoed to the lift.

The worked-out gravel pit had long since filled with water. Reeds grew along the sloping bank. A board prohibited fishing, boating and swimming. He left the inflatable rubber raft and heavy-duty canvas sack near the gate at the end of the approach lane. The sack was big enough to hold a fully-grown human body and was weighted with a manhole cover. The raft with its plug pulled out would float long enough to carry the body well out from the bank and a hundredweight of iron would hold the corpse down. If the body should be found suspicion must fall on the Koreans.

He drove across East Sussex using the byways to reach Ashdown Forest. The village was no more than a huddle of houses built around a Saxon church. A signpost behind the filling station pointed the way along a private road. It was narrow and banked with high hedges at first. A mile or so on, trees replaced the hedges, the road winding through pines and firs. Deer bounded in front of the car, disturbed by the lights and the noise. A post-and-rail fence showed ahead, enclosing part of the forest. He drove over a cattle-grid into a driveway that ended in front of a two-storey house. He stopped the engine and switched off his headlamps. The house was built in a large clearing and completely hidden in the forest except from the air. The only lights showing were downstairs.

He stuffed the snub-nosed pistol in his pocket and walked across the driveway, leaving the keys in the ignition. The front door opened as he neared. The squat unsmiling Korean was one of the two he had seen in the embassy limousine. Underwood followed him across a panelled hall hung with hunting trophies. Nam Cho was waiting in a room near the foot of the wide staircase. The door was closed on them.

'Time's important,' said Underwood. 'I'll make it as brief as I can. These people aren't fools. They know what they've got and they're not prepared to bargain. They've made that clear. It's their terms or nothing.'

'I see.' For the first time in Underwood's experience Nam Cho was showing signs of nerves. 'How do you know that they've got the book?'

'I've seen it,' said Underwood. He stepped off thin ice rapidly. 'We're not just dealing with Campbell. I think that an ex-cop called Raven is involved. He used to be on the Serious Crimes Squad. That's how he and Campbell know one another. It's Raven who's giving the orders.'

There was a bulky envelope on the table near Nam Cho's right hand.

'What's this man's motive?' he asked.

Underwood rubbed his finger and thumb together. 'Everyone's motive, money.'

Nam Cho's black eyes were bleak. 'It's a dangerous game, attributing one's own failings to others.

Money's not the only way of fulfilling one's needs. Why should Campbell need someone else?'

The curtains were undrawn, the tops of the fir trees a broken line against the sky. The house was strangely quiet.

'Because in this case the someone else is able to offer shelter, help and expert advice. Campbell has to pay this man's bill. Twenty thousand pounds.'

Nam Cho nodded. 'I have the money.'

'They want the girl and the money. Those are the terms.'

'Where is the exchange supposed to take place?'

Between the firs and the house was the pale light of the moon. An owl screeched suddenly. Underwood blinked. All this was taking longer than he had expected.

'I'm supposed to drive the girl back to my place with the money and wait there till they phone. They'll tell me where to go. It's the girl and me. Nobody else.'

Nam Cho looked up from his fingernails. 'What guarantees have you got?'

'None,' said Underwood. The balance was perfectly poised and a word either way would tip it. 'But I will be armed.'

'Who made the contact?' The envelope on the table was open. Nam Cho was checking the bundles of banknotes.

'I did,' said Underwood. 'I checked Campbell's file. There was a history of association between him and Raven and I found out where Raven lived. I guessed, the moment he picked up the phone, that Campbell was with him.'

Nam Cho seemed to withdraw his brain, his face a mask with unseeing eyes. It took him five seconds to make up his mind.

'When will the book be in my hands?'

Underwood looked at his watch. 'The sooner I'm back, the sooner they'll be in touch. They're probably watching my flat. With a man like Raven anything's possible.'

'I'll have the girl brought down,' said Nam Cho. He passed the thick envelope across the table to Underwood. 'Don't fail, Inspector Underwood. Because there's a record of every payment made to you and Drake in that book.'

112

JOHN RAVEN

July 20

He drove into the park from Knightsbridge. It was almost eight o'clock, the lights on in the lakeside restaurant, the forecourt already jammed with the vehicles of early diners. A foreign registered bus had spilled a load of tourists into the cool of the evening where they mingled with the strolling crowds. He stopped the Citroën near the call-box and switched off the engine. A couple of minutes went by before Campbell appeared, coming from the direction of the Albert Memorial. The heavy ginger stubble had gone and he was carrying a small canvas bag. He threw it into the back of the Citroën and climbed in beside Raven. His breath smelled of alcohol.

'I bought a few things. Pyjamas and a toothbrush.'

'Right,' said Raven. He'd had a drink himself. If he'd been in Campbell's place he'd probably have had more than one.

The Canadian unwrapped a stick of gum, folded it in two and stuck it in his mouth.

'Don't keep me waiting. What happened?'

Raven blew smoke through the open window. Campbell still looked tired, but his old bounce was back.

'You've been turned over,' said Raven. 'Your house is a mess, ransacked from top to bottom.'

'Did they find the book?' Campbell's eyes were anxious.

Raven tapped the front of the glove compartment.

113

'I've got it here. Tell me something. Have you been calling my number again?'

Campbell jerked his head in assent. 'I was trying to get hold of you. There's a can of *Peralite* and some caps buried in my back garden.'

'A can of *what*?' asked Raven. It sounded like a dentifrice.

'Plastic explosive,' said Campbell. 'But if I've been turned over it could be too late. I wanted to get rid of it.'

Raven pitched the cigarette end through the window. 'Forget it. Nobody dug up the garden. The important thing is that your girlfriend *wasn't* arrested.'

'I knew it,' said Campbell. 'I was right. The guy *was* a phoney.'

'You were wrong,' said Raven. 'He works on the Drugs Squad. His name's Underwood. Detective-Inspector Underwood. I had that stuff in the book translated. It's a record of Triad Society members arrested for drug offences. Then there's a list of payments made to two people over a period of thirteen months. One of them is Underwood. He's the guy who searched your house.'

'And the other one?' Campbell's gum clicked.

Raven smiled. 'The other one's an old, old friend of mine. There's other stuff mentioned. The translation runs to five or six hundred words. But this is what interests us.'

Campbell shook his head slowly. 'I don't like this business of other people being involved. It was going to be you and me.'

The light was beginning to fade. Raven switched

on his lamps. 'I promised I wouldn't do anything that would endanger your lady's safety. I haven't. I realize that the last thing we want at the moment is other people in on the act, but I had to have help.'

Campbell's jaw muscles hardened under the freckled skin. 'If she hasn't been arrested the bastards *have* got her.'

Raven's shoulders rose and fell. 'I'm afraid there's no question about it. I agree with you. The police can only make things worse for her. What's her flat-mate going to do when she finds out that Arbela doesn't come back from the police station?'

Campbell thought for a few seconds. 'She won't do anything. Not for a while, anyway. She'll probably figure that Arbela's with me and I'm one person she certainly won't call.'

Raven found another cigarette. 'You're right about sitting on something big. This *is* big.'

Campbell didn't seem to hear. 'I want Arbela out of there. We'll do a deal with the bastards.'

Raven looked at him over the flame of the lighter. 'It won't go like that. It isn't just the book that they want. They want you *and* your girl. You've seen too much and you know too much.'

'That doesn't make sense,' said Campbell. 'How are they going to get me? They don't even know where I am.'

'They don't have to,' answered Raven. 'They sit back and wait for you to offer your deal. Then they set up a meeting to which you go. The point is that you don't come back.'

The look on Campbell's face showed that Raven's words had impact.

'But what about Arbela? How do we know that she's safe?'

'She's safe enough for the moment.' It was hard to find the right words. 'We might as well get one thing out in the open. We struck a bargain.'

Campbell's smile was frosty. 'What you're trying to say is that you want your pound of flesh. You don't have to be coy about it, you know.'

Raven switched on the motor, annoyed at finding himself on the defensive. For crissakes, it *was* a bargain.

'You picked me out of the blue for reasons best known to yourself,' he said. 'We owe one another nothing. The point I'm trying to make is that whatever I said that I'd do, I will do. I expect the same from you.'

Campbell lurched as the Citroën shot forward. 'I used to think you were a regular guy. I'm beginning to change my opinion.'

Raven swung into a forbidden U-turn and headed the car south. 'It doesn't really matter too much what you think of me. I'm the only one you've got.'

Neither spoke on the way down to the Embankment. Raven was immersed in thought. He had no planned strategy in the sense that Jerry Soo would have had. He had always relied on his instinct. It had failed him on many occasions, but he had never pretended to be infallible. When sure, he was never certain. He backed the Citroën into its parking place and killed the engine. It was low tide and the stone embankment hid all but the tops of the fleet of riverboats. The sounds that he knew so well, the sounds of the life on and around the water, were

lost in the blare of the traffic. There were families
with children in the beer-garden at the back of the
pub. He pointed over at the steps cut in the
masonry.

'That's where I live. I'd like you to keep out of
sight on board.'

Campbell grinned, the class's lovable rascal taken
back into favour.

'You mean that's where I'm sleeping?'

'That's where you're sleeping. Give me a couple
of minutes then follow. I'll leave the door open. I'd
rather nobody sees you come aboard. Slam the door
behind you.'

Campbell raised his forearms from the dash.
'O.K.'

The traffic-lights were set so that you could wait
a quarter of an hour to cross the busy thoroughfare.
Raven side-stepped through the stream of speeding
cars, warding them off with an outstretched hand.
The gangway creaked gently under his weight. It
was the time of day when his neighbour walked the
Great Dane. Saul Belasus minded his own business,
but Raven drew the curtains in the bedrooms and
sitting room. He was in the kitchen when the door
on the port side opened. 'In here!' called Raven.

Campbell put his bag on a chair, his eyes curious.
Raven indicated the guest room.

'I've put a towel on your bed. We share the bathroom. Do you eat spaghetti?'

'I eat anything,' said Campbell.

Raven let the pasta fall into the boiling water and
laid the table with knives, forks and spoons. He

dished up the meal and poured a couple of bottles of *Budweiser*.

'The food's ready! ' he called.

Campbell came from the sitting room, his eyes alive with appreciation.

'I like it,' he said.

Raven pulled out a chair. 'Make the most of it. I've grown out of the habit of having people to stay.'

They ate as men do in prison mess halls, without conversation, guardians of invisibly marked territory. Raven collected the pots and pans, put them in the sink and ran scalding water over them. He found Campbell sprawled across the sofa, smoking a cheroot from Raven's box. The Canadian watched curiously as Raven lowered the arm of the record-player on a piece by Mozart. Raven sat in his chair, his brain unwinding in the rhythm of the music.

'We're going to pay a visit,' he said quietly. 'A visit to someone who doesn't know that we're coming.'

'Let me guess,' smiled Campbell. 'It's this cop you spoke about.'

'That's the order,' said Raven. 'How good are you really with locks? I mean without skeleton-keys.'

Campbell's smile faded to a look of wariness. 'That would depend on the sort of locks they were.'

'I'm talking about an ordinary suburban flat. The sort of place where the lady of the house would have her engagement ring, grandma's jet beads and the wedding presents.'

Campbell wriggled higher on the sofa. The lighting, the shape of his face and colour of hair made him look like an ageing popstar.

'I'll tell you something, friend. There isn't a lock on the market that I can't beat given time. Here, let me show you something. I need an alarm clock and a small screwdriver.' He had suddenly come alive.

Raven fetched the battered clock from the kitchen, a screwdriver from the table drawer. Campbell went to work, taking the clock to pieces. He picked two springs from the disassembled parts.

'Follow me!'

He dropped the dismembered clock in the waste bin and lighted the gas. Holding the wider spring straight, fingers at both ends, he held it over the flame. After a couple of minutes' manipulation he had a strip of steel an eighth of an inch wide. He repeated the process with the narrower spring, grinning at Raven over his shoulder.

He was clearly enjoying himself. 'Now we put the temper back.' He reheated the steel strips and plunged them into water. He switched off the sitting room lights and opened the starboard door.

'Is it all right for us to go outside?'

Raven eased past him. It was the blind side of the boat and there was nobody in sight.

'Go ahead.'

The Canadian pulled the door shut. The lock was a standard burglar-proof model, combining a springloaded tongue with a deadfall mortise. Campbell chose the narrow piece of steel and fed it into the keyhole. Raven watched fascinated as the Canadian wielded the metal strip, whistling softly. It seemed a long time before he finally straightened his back and put the flat of his hand on the door. It was open. He looked at his watch.

'Just under eight minutes. The next time it'll be four then two and then one. And if you're wondering why I bother to make keys, this is goddam hard work.'

Back in the sitting room, Raven switched on the lights again. 'What are we supposed to be looking for?' asked Campbell.

Raven removed the playing-arm from the record. 'Anything we can find. I'm betting that Underwood's our man. If he's in, we'll have to play it a different way.'

He changed into a pair of unspiked running shoes and opened his desk. The Italian automatic hadn't been fired in a year and was filthy. He gave it a perfunctory poke with a cleaning brush and checked the clip.

Campbell's face was intrigued. 'Have you got a licence for that thing?'

'I can't remember,' said Raven and that at least was honest. 'Let's hop in.'

Wimbledon Common was lonely. Raven stopped the car on the slope and switched off the lights. Mansions that had once lodged maharajahs and millionaires had been chopped into flats, the stabling and coach-houses that went with them turned into 'bijou residences'. Beyond them was a thousand acres of water, tough grass and scrub, most of it moonlit under a blue-black sky.

'O.K.,' said Raven. 'Let's make a call.'

A single call-box stood a few yards away, illuminated by a low-wattage lamp. They faced one another in the box, listening as the phone rang unanswered. They went down the hill walking side by side. The buses and cars travelling along the ridge of the common had been left a quarter of a mile away. It was still where they were, their footsteps silent in the soft dust of the bridle path. The hedges were sweet with the smell of honeysuckle. Raven halted, pointing to the stile set in the hedge. They climbed over it, coming down on to an expanse of asphalt that stretched behind the eight-storey building.

'What's his number?' asked Campbell.

'Thirty-two.'

'You want to let me take over or do you want to do this the hard way?' It was too dark where they were to see Campbell's face.

'Go ahead,' said Raven. The guy was a professional after all.

It was ten minutes before Campbell materialized suddenly from behind a parked Jaguar.

'The manager's flat is on the other side of the building. Our guy's on the third floor near the service staircase.'

Raven followed him across the hardtop and up concrete steps lighted by dim lamps. Campbell stopped on the third floor. He was wearing a pair of Raven's gloves.

'Wait here,' he warned. He pushed the swing door and vanished. Raven did his best to hear what was happening, but the noise of a nearby radio drowned everything else. Then Campbell was there, beckoning from the corridor. Raven followed him through the open door and into a hallway. The door closed and the light came on.

'Keep your voice down,' said Campbell. 'The people are in next door.'

Raven lifted his thumb. They were in a small studio flat, one room, kitchen and bath. The bed made up into a couch that was covered with an orange tweed spread. There was a cheap reproduction desk, some badly done pictures of Spain and a framed picture of a long headed man in a dark suit standing strictly to attention. There was a medal on his chest and the caption read

QUEEN'S MEDAL FOR BRAVERY August 28 1977

A slight noise turned Raven's head. Campbell was in the kitchen, standing on a chair with the window open. It was four or five feet across the well from the ledge outside to the window opening on to the service staircase. The Canadian straddled the gap, one hand hanging to a drainpipe, the other ensuring that the window was unfastened. He pulled himself back, stepped down and fastened the chain on the front door.

'Our escape route,' he said. He sat on the end of the studio couch, chewing his gum as Raven went through the contents of the desk. Underwood kept his affairs in order. There was a box-file full of receipted bills for service charges, insurance premiums. The cupro-nickel medal he had won was in a case lined with red nylon plush. Raven turned his attention to the wardrobe. An old hat box on top yielded Underwood's passport and birth certificate, a bank book showing a total of £674.98p in a deposit account and ten National Savings Certificates. The passport was valid and bore two visas, one for Tunisia, the other for Morocco. There were a number of in and out stamps, the last showing an exit from Bilbao the previous June.

Raven looked up and spread his palms. Campbell just looked. The truth was, thought Raven, he'd just found a portrait of a man with nothing to hide. A man who lived modestly, was proud of his service record and *that*, he thought, stank to high heaven. There had to be something somewhere. He searched the pockets of the suits in the closet but found nothing. A movement of Campbell's feet attracted his gaze and he saw that the couch was on rollers.

'Get your ass up!' he ordered. The Canadian did as he was told, his face puzzled. Raven pulled the couch away from the wall. Underneath was a locked leather briefcase. 'Open it,' he said to Campbell.

Campbell nodded. He straightened one of the paperclips on top of the desk and clicked off the two small brass locks.

'Help yourself,' he said to Raven.

Raven opened the case. The manila envelope inside was stuffed with hundred dollar bills and an Irish Republic passport issued the previous year in the name of Michael O'Dwyer, insurance salesman, born in Sligo. The picture on the passport was Underwood's. Underneath the manila envelope were two flight tickets. One from Heathrow to Paris, the other from Paris to Montreal. Both were for the following day. He left the things where they were and gave the briefcase to Campbell.

'Lock it up again.' He was back in the driver's seat. He put the black briefcase in the original position and pushed the bed back against the wall. The telephone was on a table near Campbell's leg, a scribbling-pad and pencil beside it. Raven switched on the goose-necked lamp. By tilting the pad in the powerful beam of light he could see the indentations left by previous writing. The name was written at an angle. *Nam Cho*. Then a scrawl as though the writer had written the words down hurriedly.

Crow's Nest, nr Coleman's Hatch. And a telephone number.

Raven looked down, his eyes locking into Campbell's. He lifted the piece of paper he'd torn from the pad.

'That's where your lady is.'

'You think so?' Campbell's whisper was nervous.

'I *know* so,' said Raven.

Campbell was up off the couch. 'Then what are we waiting for?'

They checked the room, making sure that no sign had been left of their visit and closed the kitchen window. Raven turned out the lights and took the chain off the door. They tiptoed along the corridor to the pass door. Raven refastened the window on the service staircase. There was nobody in the parking area as they climbed the stile back on to the bridle-path. Raven unlocked the Citroën. He had a hunch what Campbell was going to say and the Canadian proved him right.

'I'm going to call that number,' said Campbell. 'I'm going to offer a straight deal – the book in exchange for Arbela.'

'You're doing no such thing,' answered Raven

'Don't you realize just how lucky we've been tonight? One false move and we blow everything.'

Campbell's freckled face was pugnacious. 'Why did you leave all that stuff in the briefcase. That dude's in possession of a phoney passport. We could have his badge here and now.'

'We know what he's got,' said Raven. 'But *he* doesn't know that we know.'

'Stop being so goddam cute!' Campbell's look was frankly hostile. 'I don't give a shit about your backing and filling unless it helps me get my girl.'

'Give me time,' said Raven. 'I've told you before. She's safe just as long as we have the book.'

The pub was closing when they reached the Embankment. The river was high and the riding lights showed on the houseboats.

'More cloak-and-dagger?' Campbell's tone was sarcastic.

Raven took the key out of the ignition. 'It's been a long busy day and you're beginning to piss me off.'

'You're taking the words from my mouth,' said Campbell. 'We're not thinking along the same lines any more and it worries me.'

Raven cut the lights on the car. 'Speak your mind.'

'On the boat,' said Campbell.

Raven led the way. It was dark and unlikely that they would be seen together. He had sensed the impending showdown and had mixed feelings about it. The curtains were still drawn. He turned on the pedestal lamp. Campbell was back on the sofa, fiddling with one of the pieces of spring steel.

'Is this going to take long?' asked Raven. 'The one thing we both need is sleep.'

'I need nothing,' said Campbell. 'Neither drink sleep or bullshit. And that's what you've been giving me for the last ten hours. Pure and unadulterated bullshit.'

'So that's what you think?' said Raven.

Campbell's eyes were steady. 'That's what I think, my friend. I came to you out of desperation. There was literally nobody else I could go to. You had the reputation of being straight, of keeping your word once you gave it. O.K. So you made it plain earlier that you owe me nothing. I accept that. You've got your own reasons for helping me and you haven't really told me what they are. Like this, I don't know what I'm committed to.'

Raven sighed, moved by the other man's frankness. 'Suppose I gave you my reasons for doing what I'm doing. Would that make any difference?'

'Try me,' said Campbell. 'Mine are simple. I happen to be in love.'

'Are you sure about that?'

Campbell put both feet down very deliberately. 'I don't think that's any of your business. Added to which I don't think you're competent to judge.'

Raven nodded. 'Perhaps not. I'm sorry.'

'I don't really care what makes you tick,' said Campbell. 'Or whether or not you believe that I'm in love with Arbela. Her life's in danger because of me and I want to make sure that you're not playing games with us.'

Raven poured himself a drink. Campbell shook his head.

'You're right and I'm wrong,' said Raven. 'I ought to have told you before, but I wasn't a hundred per cent sure. I am now. I was a cop for nearly eighteen years. I didn't fit in very well for lots of reasons. I never believed that a halo was issued with a warrant card. I knew there were dishonest judges and policemen just as there were thieves who were honest. The dividing line seemed arbitrary. I want you to believe that I can't recall doing anything as a cop that I'm ashamed of.'

He stopped, disliking the sound of what he'd just said in spite of its truth.

'I'm listening,' Campbell reminded.

'During my last few years on the Force one man did his best to destroy me. He disliked everything about me. The way I did my job, the way I talked and dressed. He even resented this boat. He got it in his head that I was an affront to the decent Old Bills, men like himself who'd grown up on fish-and-chips and who picked their noses at breakfast. Fair enough. Everyone has the right to like or dislike, but this one pulled rank, lied and did his best to set me up. He used anything he could find in the Dirty Tricks Department. So finally I resigned. He's still at the Yard, dug in deeper than a bog rat, one of the Establishment. Commander Drake. I always suspected that the bastard was bent. Today I had the proof. Underwood was always his boy and he still is. I believe in miracles, Campbell and I want Drake. There's nothing more to be said.'

He carried his empty glass to the kitchen. When he came back into the sitting room, Campbell's face was thoughtful.

'O.K., Raven. It's time for me to level with you. When we came back here tonight I'd already made up my mind I was going to take your gun and your car and the book and go down to Sussex.'

Raven shook his head. 'You wouldn't have made it alone.'

'You may be right at that,' said Campbell. 'So I'm going to make a proposition. Man to man.'

'Tell me,' said Raven.

'Help me and I'll help you. But Arbela has to come first. I want to go down to that house tonight. When we leave she comes with us. One way or another, she comes with us. If we can do that you've got my word I'll go the limit with you. Between us we'll straighten out this fucker Drake and anyone else you want. Here's my hand on it.'

Raven took it, certain now that his impulse was right. 'O.K. We'll do it your way. These people may be untouchable, but there's a limit to what they can do. This house in the country isn't sovereign territory. Sooner or later we're going to need outside help. There's someone I'd trust with my life. He already knows something of what's going on. I say we ought to talk to him.'

'A cop?'

'Yes,' said Raven.

'I'm not having cops in the act till Arbela's safe.' Campbell said obstinately.

Raven was sweating, but it was excitement not fear. 'I've given my word about that. We can trust this man.'

Campbell's mood changed suddenly and he

grinned. 'Go ahead and call him. I think I'll take that drink you offered.'

He poured one and sank it in a gulp.

'I'd watch it with that stuff,' said Raven.

Campbell nodded. 'We've got to get her out of there.'

'We will,' promised Raven. The truth was that he was playing a hunch. There was no certainty of anything. But he'd waited too long for Drake for anything else to go wrong. He dialled Soo's number and Louise answered.

'It's John,' said Raven. 'I'm sorry about this, darling. I know its late but I have to talk to Jerry.'

Soo came on the line. 'Get a pencil and paper,' said Raven. 'And take this down. Coleman's Hatch. c-o-l-e-m-a-n s h-a-t-c-h. It's in East Sussex between a place called Wych Cross and Upper Hartfield. Have you got that?'

'Got it,' said Soo.

'There's a house called Crows Nest in the area that's either rented or owned by the North Korean Embassy. That's where we're going now. If you don't hear from me by six tomorrow morning notify the local police and don't take no for an answer. I'll be in trouble, Jerry.'

He could hear the sound of the radio playing in the background, his friend's breathing.

'Don't do it,' said Soo. 'Get in your car and come over here. Let me handle things now. You're in no position to break the law.'

'I'm in no position if I don't,' said Raven. 'Just do as I say, Jerry.'

He put the phone down quickly. It rang immediately. He took the receiver off the rest and left it there.

Campbell was watching him closely. 'Have you got any ordnance survey maps?'

'In the cupboard under the record shelves.' He pointed. Campbell pulled out the boxed set of linen-backed maps while Raven fetched an anorak from his bedroom. The Italian gun and a pair of wire-cutters weighted the pockets of the anorak.

He squatted on the floor next to Campbell. The village they wanted was tiny, the house marked as being in a clearing a couple of miles into the forest. Raven lifted his eyes from the map.

'There's only one way into the place and don't forget there's a moon.'

Campbell's sandy hair flopped as he leaned forward tracing a serpentine line with his forefinger. It led from the A22 through the forest to a point near the house.

'How about this?'

The only reference was that the track belonged to the Forestry Commission. It was probably used by tractors. There was no way of knowing whether a car would be able to handle it. In their favour were the facts that the ground was dry and the Citroën had a high clearance. He folded the map and put it back in its case.

'We'd better move.'

It was well after ten when they drove into the hamlet. A church and a pub sandwiched two rows of cottages. The place looked dead, the pub and the filling station closed for the night. A sign behind the filling station read

They drove on, taking the road that skirted the southern periphery of the forest, to the road that ran north and south. A fast five miles took them to the spot they had seen on the map. There was no gate, no wire, just a gently climbing track with the cold light of the moon laying shadows across it. Raven turned the Citroën off the road and cut his headlamps. After five hundred yards, the forest swallowed them completely. The only sound was the purr of the engine. The track swung and straightened continually, the divergencies marked by piles of felled trees, lopped ready for hauling. Raven was watching the speedometer. The track had measured four miles on the map. They'd already travelled three and a half. The end came abruptly with no thinning of the fir trees, the track simply widening into a semicircle that offered a tractor room to turn. There was enough space for Raven to manoeuvre the Citroën so that its nose faced the road. They walked east in Indian file with Raven leading. Neither spoke as they crossed the thick layers of fir needles. The trees grew closer, blotting out the light of the moon till at last they were walking in darkness.

A loud shriek came unexpectedly from the branches over their heads followed by the heavy whirr of an owl in flight. Raven waded forward into bracken till barbed wire snagged his trousers. He used the cutters on it, severing the five strands. The bracken ended with the trees, suddenly, leaving them standing on the edge of a cabbage-patch that had gone to seed. The rest of the kitchen garden was over-grown.

They walked forward cautiously towards the back of a stone-built house showing over the roofs of the outbuildings. There was a light in the second floor, the curtains drawn behind what looked like barred windows. Campbell's fingers closed on Raven's arm as a woman's shape showed beyond the curtains.

'That's Arbela,' he whispered hoarsely.

GEORGE DRAKE

July 20

There were garden gnomes in front of the ugly two bedroom house. The half-coconut dangling from a wire was supposed to attract the blue-tits. She hadn't even bothered to move the water sprinkler. It was where he had left it at half past eight that morning, the ground around completely saturated. He left the car on the kerb, unfastened the gate and switched off the sprinkler. He let himself quietly into the hall with its permanent smell of camphor and furniture polish. Most of the things in the house had been bought right at the beginning with Mildred's money providing the down-payments. Money saved working on a soft-touch factory job while he was up to his ass in sand and mosquitoes servicing tanks in the desert.

The curtains were drawn in the unused sitting room. She worried about things like carpets fading and put antimacassars on the backs of armchairs no one ever sat in. And that bloody bell round the neck of the cat. It eyed him now from the kitchen table, its tail lashing. His wife's voice came from her bedroom.

'That you, George?'

He hung his battered black Homburg on a hook. When he turned, she was standing at the top of the stairs. A weekly visit to the hairdresser kept her blonde, but she'd thrown in the towel against obesity years ago. She was wearing slippers, a baby-blue wrapper over her flabby body and she was wheezing.

She'd been wheezing for the last six months though she always denied it. Wheezing and hawking and spitting all night long.

She looked down at him, smiling. 'You're early, aren't you?'

Or late. Or on time. Conversation was made from the fact of putting your foot through the door.

'There's a conference in Glasgow,' he said. 'I'll be away for two or three days.'

The breath bubbled in her lungs and she pressed a hand to her chest.

'That's nice, dear. Did you tell the man about the washing-machine?'

It would have been the same had he told her he'd lost both his legs.

'He's coming tomorrow morning.'

But she was already out of earshot, the sound turned up on the television. At six o'clock she'd dress and go to her sister's place in Croydon, returning after supper to sneak the last gin from the bottle she kept under her bed. They had slept in separate bedrooms for the last thirteen years. He went up to his own room and packed a small bag. He took his passport and the fifty pounds cash they kept in the house in case of an emergency. He poked his head through her doorway. The window was open, but the room still smelled faintly of gin. She smiled up at him.

'You're off then, are you?'

He touched her broken-veined cheek with his lips. 'I won't bother phoning.'

'No dear, take care,' she answered mechanically, her eyes on the television screen.

He took one last look at the foot of the stairs, the

cat giving him stare for stare. He'd been waiting for this moment for twenty-three years and at last it was here. Twenty-three years ago, sitting behind the steamed windows of a café in Hatton Garden on a raw day in January. He was forty-two years old, a detective on the Flying Squad, not the new lot, but the old time Heavy Mob. Barney Mendoza had shambled up to the table and placed an envelope containing eighteen hundred pounds on the seat. Pounds were still worth money in those days and the sum had paid off his mortgage. That was his first bribe. He was green at the game, but hungry. He'd learned quickly. Position was everything. The trick was to be where the action was. His take increased with his expertise. He'd survived a departmental inquiry over the years, coming out of it with a promotion that marked his complete vindication. It was possible that he could have survived this new threat, but he'd no intention of putting it to the test. The red signals were up everywhere. He was leaving nothing behind. The house had been in Mildred's name for the last ten years and there was enough money in the joint deposit account to keep her in gin and cat food for the rest of her life.

He'd always lived modestly, within his salary as a policeman. Even the paid-off mortgage had been accounted for by a win on the football pools. The real amount had been no more than a couple of hundred pounds. He'd multiplied this sum by ten. In any case the figures were confidential. Every penny he had taken illegally over the years had been banked in different accounts all over the country. Four in London, others in Bristol, Coventry, Bath and Ipswich. His last overall balance showed him to be worth just under £273,000.

He had accepted the risk of detection right from the beginning. His early-warning system had been designed to give him enough time to clear his bank accounts and still be ahead of the chase. But he had seen too many certainties go wrong in his time and devised a second line of retreat. The scene in the canteen that morning had deeply disturbed him. A discreet telephone call warned him that the red lights were shining everywhere. There was no time to close his accounts and run. He'd leave that to Underwood who was going to run in any case. Underwood looked and played the part, but deep down he was chicken. He'd stampede. There was no question about it and they'd probably nail him on his way out.

Drake's smile was conscious recognition of his own foresight. His alternative plan was almost as good as the first choice.

He closed the garden gate quietly on the gnomes, the cat and on Mildred. It would be months now before his new life began but he was even looking forward to the waiting period. He only wished that he could have seen their faces when they heard of his disappearance. The ones who sat in high places, the bastards he'd had to con and fight ever since his rookie days, the smooth ones with their old-school tie freemasonry. The gentlemen who patronized the Camberwell boy who put vinegar on his chips and slept with his socks on.

He drove to Charing Cross Station, left his car in the hotel forecourt and walked through to the booking hall. He bought a day return on the Seaspeed hovercraft. Folkstone to Boulogne. Then he changed station and ticket office. This time it was a one-way ticket to Paris via Dover and Calais. Two and a half hours later he was at Dover hoverport. The next flight was ready to load.

He presented his passport. *George Drake Occupation Police Officer born Camberwell, London, 8 February 1912.*

He smiled, arranging his mouth in the square shape that was supposed to indicate good humour and passed through the barrier, a burly figure with steel grey hair and eyes like hatpins, a figure likely to be remembered among the twenty-odd passengers who were travelling with him. He made himself noticed on the half hour trip, opening windows, managing to mention his destination as he bought unwanted duty free goods from the hostess. He was first off the craft on the landing-pad, first through passport control and customs and on to the Paris express that was waiting. The arrival of the hover-craft coincided with that of the cross-channel ferry. A couple of hundred people surged forward to board the train. Porters were wheeling baggage, harassed mothers looking for straying children. There was a group of nuns and campers carrying their gear.

He left the duty free scotch on the rack and made his way along the corridor to the back of the train. The barrier was ten yards away, the traffic coming in. He shoved through, using his shoulders and waving his ticket at the official. Minutes later he was sitting in a public lavatory near the *Places des Nations,* a small mirror hanging on the back of the door. He took a bottle of Quik Tan and cotton-wool from his bag and started working the lotion into his face, hands and neck, taking care with the leathery seams and the spaces between his fingers. He exchanged the shiny blue suit for a pair of cord trousers and an old jacket decorated with a couple of burrs. He took off his tie. Stout walking boots, metal-rimmed spectacles and the identity card he had had for three years finished the change of personality. William Thompson, aged sixty-four, retired caretaker back from a day on the Continent. He left the lavatories carrying the bag with his old clothing. Twenty minutes' sharp walking took him to the outskirts of the town, sand-dunes and salt-water creeks. He clambered down off the road under the swooping screaming gulls. He weighted the bag with stones and watched it sink. Then carefully, page by page and using a box of matches, he burned his passport.

A taxi took him the eighteen miles to Boulogne where he joined the group of people waiting for the last Hovercraft, presenting his identity-card and the return half of the excursion ticket. A couple of the men passengers had drunk too much wine. It was getting late and day trippers were just about the bottom of the travelling bag. Customs and passport control hurried them through and out of the Hovercraft building. Instead of joining the train for London, Drake walked the half-mile into the town and boarded a National coach. There was nothing in the newspaper he bought in the coach station. He closed his eyes and composed himself for the three-hour journey. The blank-shielded signet ring on his left hand was deeply embedded in the flesh. He'd have to cut it off.

He'd learned a lot from the Lucan affair. The worldwide publicity and search had made a big impression on him. Notoriety and the promise of a large reward put the sort of pressure on a fugitive that was hard to resist. Once your face was in the newspapers, a price placed on your capture, every knucklehead in every bar, every cab-driver, chambermaid and waiter, was in there with eyes on stalks looking for the reward money.

In his case there'd be plenty of notoriety and without doubt a reward. The newspaper reporters would be on his tail. After all, they'd already been to Brazil in search of one of the Great Train Robbers. They'd go as far for him when the full story broke and the best of British luck to them.

He catnapped all the way to Victoria Coach Station, his brain dozing, but his senses alert. He walked out of the bus terminal on to Buckingham Palace Road and bought another newspaper on the corner. There was nothing in it to worry him. The Underground took him to Marble Arch where he surfaced and walked west on Bayswater Road as far as the giant greystone complex near Albion Gate. The apartment block was built in the form of an H with floral gardens and ornamental ponds filling the spaces between the lateral bars. There were ten entrances, two at the end of each wing and two in the middle. Only one of these was staffed. The building was popular with the Japanese and Arabs, the rentals mostly temporary. The transient tenants came and went.

He took the lift to the fourth floor. The corridor was empty as he let himself into the flat. There was no post in the box. He would have been alarmed if there had been. It was four months since he'd been in the flat and the air was stale. He turned on the conditioning unit. Two sets of curtains hung in the sitting room windows. Across Bayswater Road was the Park, but even with a pair of field-glasses it would have been impossible for anyone to see through the close-meshed net.

He had rented the flat five years before, using the name Humphrey Bates, born in Brighton, an emigrant to New Zealand who'd done well as a master-builder. Bates came to England once a year to enjoy the cricket, Henley and Ascot. The name and background were genuine. So was the New Zealand passport in the bureau drawer. The difference was that the passport bore Drake's picture, albeit with spectacles. The real Bates had died in a car crash in Norway some years before. The Norwegian police had returned the passport to Scotland Yard where Drake had acquired it.

The service bills were paid by banker's order. In all the time Drake had been a tenant he had never seen a porter nor used the main entrance. Experience had told him that the place to hide was not in some lonely farmhouse with curious or friendly neighbours. The place to be was in the heart of a great city. Nobody in the building knew his face, even as Bates. No one ever came to the flat. There was no reason for anyone to come to the flat.

He had taken the place as it stood, furnished and curtained, having seen it from the outside and hearing the estate agent's inventory read over the phone. The keys had been sent to a firm of lawyers.

The hunt would die down and there'd be other people to chase. After a while he would venture out, taking the train to one bank after another. He had made a habit of making large cash deposits and withdrawals, switching the sums from one account to the other. There was no danger of a bank manager becoming curious. Once the accounts were cleared, he would hibernate. The store cupboards and deep-freeze were loaded with enough food to keep him for four or five months and if he ran short of anything he could always slip out and replenish supplies in one of the local supermarkets.

He soaked in the bath, glad that things had finally come to a head. It was odd the way he had hung on when he no longer had to. Greed, possibly. Or maybe it was the feeling he got when those snotty-nosed superintendents gave him the salute, the 'Good *morning*, Commander!' Good morning, bullshit! They hated his guts the lot of them.

He dried himself, put on the silk pyjamas and cashmere robe and cut himself a plate of smoked salmon. Then he uncorked a half-bottle of Roederer. From now on this was what life would be like, everything that they thought he didn't understand, everything that he'd waited for. He smiled to himself and switched on the portable TV set. Sound-proofed doors and windows were a feature of the complex.

'In for the night,' as Mildred always said. In fact it was in for a number of nights.

JOHN RAVEN

July 20–21

It was hard to tell whether the figure behind the
lighted curtain was that of a man or a woman, but
Raven pinned his faith to Campbell's hunch. The
light went out in the window as they watched.
Campbell's grip tightened on Raven's arm.

'That was Arbela!'

They were crouching on their heels, their backs
against the brickwork of the stables. Lights still
shone in the kitchen and at the front of the house.

'We've got to know how many people are in
there,' whispered Raven. 'You take the back. Keep
your head down and use your ears as well as your
eyes. We want to know *where* they are as well.'

He glanced back from the shelter of the fir trees
that bordered the lawn, but Campbell was one with
the night. The curtains were partly drawn in the
room overlooking the drive, making it difficult for
him to see at the angle at which he was standing. A
glimmer of reflected light illuminated the transom
over the front door. The other windows in the front
were in darkness. He tiptoed across the drive,
approaching the parked car from the blind side.
The door was open, the keys dangling in the dash.
He slid into the front seat and felt for the catch on
the glove compartment. The flap dropped. The
space was empty. He swivelled his body sideways.
The radio equipment was standard for a police vehicle used in Danger Area operations. The shortwave
phone was for car-to-car communication, the second

for long-range hook-ups. It was tempting to take the ignition keys with him, but he left them and moved to the back of the car, his lanky body bent awkwardly. He had a better view now through the curtains. The Korean was sitting with his back to the window, his left forearm resting on the table, a bulky envelope near his elbow. Underwood was doing the talking, gesticulating, his narrow head cocked. Raven crossed the hardtop to the front door and laid his ear against the crack. He heard two men talking. A smell of cooking drifted out, reminding him of a Chinese restaurant.

Campbell was waiting behind the stables, his whisper hoarse. 'I've got two, that's all. Both in the kitchen. The chauffeur and the security guard.'

Raven crouched beside him. 'I've got two more. Nam Cho and Underwood. The squad car in the front has to be his.'

The bedroom window was still in darkness. Raven had pledged his word, but he still didn't have the answer. A direct assault on the house would be crazy. Even if they could find the tools required and a ladder, any attempt to break through the grille work on Arbela's window was bound to be heard. And there was the risk to the girl's life, which was very real. The first sign of danger and the Koreans would use her as a shield.

He straightened up, pointing towards the fringe of forest. 'There's a phone at the end of the lane. We've got to take a chance here.'

The house stood silent in the moonlight, a stage set waiting for the players to make their entrances. The two men worked their passage through the bracken taking the shortest way to the lighted 'phone box. Raven reached up and unscrewed the lamp from its socket. It was an old fashioned call-box. Calls had to go through the operator.

'This is a gamble,' he said. 'So keep your fingers crossed. With any sort of luck it should work.'

Campbell's bounce seemed to have vanished. 'And if it doesn't?'

'We'll try it your way,' said Raven and asked for the numbers.

It was some time before a curt voice said 'Yes?'

Raven's tone and accent changed convincingly. 'East Sussex Constabulary, Inspector Bailey speaking. I'd like to talk to a Mr Nam Cho.'

The reply was suddenly hesitant. 'I'm afraid Mr Nam Cho isn't available.'

Raven's hunch was that he was already talking to him. 'I see. You don't know where the gentleman is?'

'I'm afraid not. Can I help you in any way?'

Raven leaked caution into his answer. 'It's a rather delicate matter, sir.'

'That's all right. I work for Mr Nam Cho.'

It was close in the box but Raven kept the door closed. A sound from the woods might betray him. He gave an embarrassed laugh.

'We've had an inquiry from the Met, that's the police in London, sir. It's about a Mrs Arbela Stewart. The lady's been reported as missing.'

'*Missing?* I'm afraid I don't understand. How does that concern Mr Nam Cho?'

Raven cleared his throat. 'I believe the lady's flatmate referred to an abduction, sir.'

144

The phone went dead, but only temporarily. 'I don't know if you realize this, Inspector, but Mr Nam Cho is a diplomat.'

'I do indeed, sir.' Raven rushed the words. 'We wouldn't want to embarrass the gentleman in any way, of course. I'm told that Mrs Stewart works as a secretary for the North Korean Embassy. There's probably some mistake.'

The caller laughed easily. 'Well I can put your mind to rest about one thing, Inspector. The lady you're looking for isn't here.'

'No, sir. It's rather what I expected, but we have to do our job. There's obviously some confusion somewhere. I'm sorry to have troubled you. Goodnight, sir.' He replaced the phone and shouldered the door open.

'Move!'

They raced back down the lane. Moonlight picked out the metal slats of the cattle grid. The white entrance gate was open. Raven closed it. The driveway curved sharply to the right. He wiped the sweat from his neck, looking towards the house. The minutes stretched till he heard the sound he was waiting for. A car had started up at the other end of the driveway. Its headlamps lighted the serried fir trees. The car came fast around the bend with Underwood at the wheel, Arbela's frightened face a blob beside him. He hit the brakes seeing the closed gate from twenty yards away. The brakes held in time for Underwood to wrestle the car to a halt, but too late for him to defend himself.

Raven wrenched the car door open and jammed his gun against Underwood's throat. The engine had stalled. Campbell was over by the gate, staring blindly into the beam from the headlamps as Arbela ran towards him. The Canadian unfastened the gate. He and the girl climbed into the back of the car. Raven motioned Underwood to move over. He took a gun from the cop's pocket, an envelope from the glove compartment. He passed these back to Campbell who was sitting with an arm around Arbela's shoulder. Raven switched on the engine and the tyres whispered down the tarmac. He was hitting fifty miles an hour by the time he reached the junction with the London Road. He glanced up in the rear-view mirror. 'All right?'

Arbela's eyes were wet, but she was smiling. 'All right.'

Raven turned his attention to Underwood. 'You'd better get ready to do some talking.'

The lights ahead belonged to a café and petrol station. The parking space out front was half-filled with long-distance trucks. Raven pulled the car off the road and drove in behind a ten-tonner with Spanish number plates and a load of citrus fruit. The teenager working the pumps had his ear stuck to a transistor radio. There was no one else in sight. Raven cut the engine.

Underwood's gaze shifted in a face hacked out of stone, a man running scared and devoid of hope. Campbell was leaning forward, holding the gun to the back of the policeman's neck. Arbela had straightened her hair and was smoking, her eyes watching Raven.

'Well now, Detective-Inspector,' he said comfortably. 'It looks to me as if you're on a fast downhill run to nowhere.'

The worm under the skin in the middle of Underwood's forehead beat time with the pulse in his throat. The back of his hand was bleeding where he had caught it during the near-crash earlier. The tip of his tongue flickered over his lips, but he stayed silent.

'You'll talk,' Raven assured him. 'People like you always do, sooner or later. I want Drake. Are you with me?'

Campbell dug the barrel of Underwood's gun deeper into the cop's flesh, giving emphasis to Raven's question. Underwood's head lifted.

'I know who you are.'

'Good for you.' Raven's smile was encouraging. 'I was going to tell you anyway. You're not going to walk, that's for sure. But you can still do yourself some good. I want Drake in a cell and you're going to give me the key. Names, dates, places. Anything that will put him there.'

'You're Raven,' challenged Underwood.

The smoke from Arbela's cigarette drifted in front of Raven. 'That's right,' he said. 'Maybe not the smartest cop in the world, but a stubborn fucker. You can do this one of two ways, Detective-Inspector. With help or without.'

Underwood's eyes swivelled sideways. A car was pulling away from the pumps. The policeman's eyes followed it longingly.

'I'll take the help,' he said quietly.

Raven moved his head up and down. 'I thought you would. You've been in the business as long as

I was and you know what's needed. Think of Drake as a client. A villain you're going to stitch up. So no holds are barred, O.K.?'

Underwood moulded his narrow features into an expression of cunning.

'I still want to know what the help's going to be.'

Raven waved a hand. 'Put the gun away,' he said to Campbell. 'He's not going anywhere. There's nowhere for him to go.'

The Canadian stuffed the snub-nosed revolver in the waistband of his trousers. Raven looked at Underwood thoughtfully.

'I'll tell you what the help's going to be. You're getting the chance to stand up in court and put Drake away. Maybe you'll tell the truth and maybe you'll lie. But you'll make it stick. It just might make the difference between five and fifteen years. And that's a lot of years, Underwood.'

Diesel fumes belched as the Spanish truck moved out, leaving them exposed. The café was still fairly full, rock music blasting across the forecourt.

Underwood lifted his shoulders. 'It doesn't look as if I've got any choice, does it?'

'You never did,' said Raven. 'Better make the most of whatever you do have.'

He turned, facing the pair in the back. They were sitting very close to one another, the bulky envelope on the seat next to Campbell.

'Open it!' said Raven.

The Canadian tore the flap with a forefinger, whistling as he stared down at the contents. He showed Raven the sheaves of twenty and ten pound notes. Raven took the envelope. The money wasn't

Underwood's and the Koreans weren't likely to claim it. Maybe once in a lifetime a man had the chance to play Fairy Godfather. He stuffed the envelope in his shirt and reached for the long-distance radio-phone. The words came easily from memory.

'Code twenty-six and fourteen. Detective-Inspector Underwood.' He gave the operator Jerry Soo's home number. It was a full two minutes before it answered. Raven spoke rapidly.

'It's all over, Jerry. I'm calling from Underwood's car. The girl's safe and so's Campbell. They're here with me. The Koreans are probably running, but we've got the book and Underwood's pulling the plug on Drake. Did you get that last bit, Jerry?'

'I got it, yes. Just where are you?'

Raven told him. 'I want you to set up a top level conference. Get the Commissioner out of his bed. Jerry?'

Soo's voice sounded through an unstifled yawn. 'I heard you. The Commissioner out of his bed. Louise is saying that she doesn't love you any more. And that goes for me.'

'You'll both change your mind when you're promoted,' said Raven. Underwood was following the conversation, his face without expression. 'It's the big one, Jerry,' Raven went on. 'The one we've been waiting for and I'm relying on you.'

Soo's second yawn was even louder. 'That's what worries me. If anything goes wrong it's back to the steam-iron for me. You realize that, I suppose?'

Behind the kidding was the assurance that the help Raven needed would be provided.

'I'll bring you my laundry,' he answered.

Soo's voice took on new urgency. 'How soon will you be at the Yard?'

'An hour,' said Raven. 'And get someone out to Underwood's place. There's a briefcase under his bed that we'll want.' He smiled over the phone at Underwood. 'And, Jerry!'

'Make it quick. There's a lot to do.'

'When they go for Drake I want to be there. I don't care how you fix it as long as it's done.'

London was a waste of empty streets where strobe lights blinked in endless shop fronts. It was just after three by Big Ben as they drove over Westminster Bridge. Raven turned the car left into Victoria Street. A few taxis were scooting in both directions carrying late night revellers homeward. New Scotland Yard was ablaze, grey and ever-vigilant. *Business twenty-four hours a day. We never close.*

He stopped in front of the main entrance. The desks in the Reception Area were unmanned. Three plainclothesmen were lolling on a bench in the hall while behind them a couple of uniformed men guarded the lifts. Raven switched off the engine.

'It's three o'clock in the morning,' he said to Underwood. 'And we're home. Don't have me chasing you up and down the streets.'

Underwood's gaze slid from the building in front of them back to Raven. His voice was bitter.

'I'm beginning to believe all the things they say about you.'

'They're probably true,' Raven said cheerfully.

He twisted his neck, speaking to the couple on the back seat. 'Stay in the car.'

Frown lines creased the corners of Campbell's eyes and his arm encircled Arbela protectively.

'We're dead on our feet, man!'

And scared, thought Raven, smelling the other man's fear. 'I won't be a second,' he promised.

He leaned across Underwood and released the doorcatch. 'Straight up the steps. You know the way.'

He was close behind Underwood as they went through the glass doors, meeting the challenge of three pairs of eyes. It was the first time he had been inside the building for three years. The nearest plainclothesman wore trendy clothes and a swash-buckling beard. His recognition of Underwood was the barest flicker.

'Can I help you?' he said to Raven.

Raven inclined his head. Contempt for Under-wood, resentment for the outsider allowed back in, both were discreetly displayed in the man's manner.

'My name's Raven. Detective-Inspector Soo is expecting me.' The other two plainclothesmen drifted nearer the doors. The bearded one put his plastic cup on the bench.

'And this gentleman?'

This time he looked at Underwood as he would have done a stranger.

Raven grinned. 'Either he's turning himself in or I'm making what I believe is called a citizen's arrest. You can take your pick. Just as long as you keep an eye on him. Two minutes.'

He passed through the glass doors outstaring the

151

two men standing there. He could hear Soo's name being called on the P.A. system behind him. Campbell and Arbela were as he had left them, close and apprehensive. Raven slid into the driving seat.

'I want you people to listen to me carefully. Time's running out on you both. The Koreans will never go for trial and nor will you. This could be your last chance. Take it.'

He pulled out the fat envelope stuffed with banknotes and dropped it in Arbela's lap. She stared down at it as though her knees had suddenly burst into flames.

'I never saw this before,' he went on. 'If the money ever existed it must have been left in the house.'

She still made no move to touch the envelope. He craned across and put it in her handbag.

'There are times when you don't ask questions, Arbela. And this is one of them.'

She hesitated for a second then lifted his hand and pressed it against her cheek. 'I'll do it,' she said.

Campbell's expression was baffled. 'I don't know what to say,' he muttered.

'To me, nothing,' said Raven. 'Get him out of the country,' he added to Arbela. 'If you're still here by tomorrow night I'm going to be on your tail.'

Campbell fumbled the door catch. 'Let's go,' he said hurriedly.

They moved off up the street, half-running as the lights of a cruising taxi showed at the intersection. Raven went back inside. The entrance hall was deserted. One of the security guards opened the lift.

'Inspector Soo is waiting for you in the Commissioner's office, sir.'

'How about the others?' Raven's hand indicated the empty hall.

'They're all upstairs, sir.' The man thumbed the express button and the cage rose swiftly. His voice was respectful as the lift doors reopened. 'On your right, sir.'

A deep pile carpet absorbed the sound of Raven's coming. Two of the plainclothesmen from downstairs were waiting for him. One of them opened the office door. There were four people in the room. Underwood, the trendy detective, Jerry Soo in jeans and sneakers and, behind the desk, the Commissioner.

The curtains were undrawn. The illuminated dial of Big Ben showed half past three. Soo's smile flashed on and off, his pebble-black eyes indicating caution.

'This is Mr Raven, sir. Underwood's already made a partial statement.'

'Yes,' said Grandy.

Raven took a better look at him. The clown had actually said *yerss*. Grandy was smooth-haired with a matinée idol's moustache and flared nostrils. If he'd been called from his bed, his attire showed no sign of it. There was a flower in his well-cut jacket. He showed a set of long smokers' teeth.

'I understand you used to be on the Force yourself, Mr Raven?' The tone of voice and manner were condescending.

'I try to forget it,' said Raven.

Grandy frowned. 'According to Detective-Inspector Soo here you seem to have played a major role in all this drama. Almost an instigator, as it were. Why didn't you see fit to bring the matter to the attention of the proper authorities – I mean right at the beginning?'

Raven lighted a cigarette, his delay in answering deliberate. He'd suffered too much to take this sort of put-down without fighting back.

'That's easy. The proper authorities were the police. Going to them didn't make sense since two senior policemen were involved in various sorts of felony. It was difficult to know who to trust. I decided to wait for the *fait accompli* if you take my meaning, Mr Grandy.'

A faint flush invaded Grandy's well-shaven cheek. '*Colonel* Grandy if you don't mind. You realize of course that as a result of these serious allegations the Foreign Office has been alerted?'

'I should have thought that elementary,' said Raven. Soo's eyes were still signalling danger, but the moment was too sweet not to make the most of it. 'You'll find that Detective-Inspector Underwood's able to supply you with enough information to have Nam Cho and his colleagues thrown out of the country. But your best bet, of course, is going to be Commander Drake. A simple and old-fashioned story of bribery, corruption and nepotism. You'll love it.'

Grandy cocked his head like the hammer of a pistol. 'You understand, I hope that if any of the allegations you've made prove to be without foundation you'll be in serious trouble.'

It was Raven's turn to redden under his suntan.

'Look at it the other way. If they turn out to be true, *you're* the one in trouble.'

Grandy swung on the bearded detective, looking at Underwood. 'Put this bugger in a cell. Get his full statement, signed, and lock him up. I want no one going near him after that until I give the order. Understood?'

'Understood, sir.' The door closed on Underwood and his escort.

Jerry Soo moved a little closer to Raven, whatever he wanted to say still unsaid. Grandy's voice had a certain amount of satisfaction.

'Some of your charges are going to be difficult to substantiate, Mr Raven. I'm talking about the ones against Commander Drake. It isn't that he may not be guilty. But he left the country this afternoon.'

The sound of a church clock somewhere near broke the sudden hush in the room. Raven looked at Soo, shaking his head.

'I don't believe it.' The words were more of a plea than a statement.

Soo turned his hands over, palms upwards. Grandy looked at his watch.

'It doesn't seem to matter really what you believe, Mr Raven. Not in this context anyway. We'll let you know if and when we need you. The Inspector will help you find your way out.'

They walked along the deserted corridor. Neither man spoke as the lift descended. They emerged into a hall where a shouting Arab was brandishing a long blond wig. Its transvestite owner stood bald-headed and haughty under the lights, wearing a black pencil line skirt and half-inch false eyelashes.

The argument was being refereed by one of the plainclothesmen who had been outside the Commissioner's office. Soo opened the glass door to the street. They walked a block to the café on the corner. The chairs were up on the table, a mop ready in a pail of soapy water. A pair of homeward bound hookers occupied two of the four bar stools, chatting to the Greek proprietor.

Soo planted a couple of chairs and the Greek brought them coffee.

'Closing in ten minutes, Mister Inspector.'

The hookers slid from their seats in unison. One looked back from the doorway.

'You're getting a low class of customer, Sam.'

The Greek shrugged and flapped his cloth at the top of the table.

'I been trying to get rid of them two slags for last half-an-hour. The coffee's on me.'

He reversed the OPEN sign hanging in the door and retired to the kitchen. Raven stared down at his cup. He felt drained and defeated, like an outpunched and outsmarted fighter asked to come up for yet another round.

'I don't believe it,' he repeated. 'Drake wouldn't take-off like that. He couldn't have known that I was on to Underwood.'

Soo knuckled his blueblack bristle. 'I had to give Grandy the full strength over the phone. He *was* in bed when I called.'

Raven sipped the coffee glumly. The Greek was making himself a bacon sandwich and the smell reminded Raven that it was a long time since he had eaten.

'Drake must have been tipped off.' His voice was suddenly loud and Soo shook his head warningly.

'What happened to the girl and Campbell?' the Chinese asked.

'They're going back to Canada,' said Raven, reaching in his pocket for a cigarette. His gun was heavy against his thigh and he remembered that Campbell must still have Underwood's weapon. 'At least that was the general idea.'

Soo stretched across the table and took the tipped cigarette from Raven's mouth.

'Wrong end. Do you really think those kids'll make out?'

'Who knows, Jerry.' Raven thought about it a little more without success. 'Who the fuck knows. You do what you can.'

'*You* do,' said Soo.

The Greek was grinning at them from the kitchen doorway. There was bacon-grease on his chin.

'I've got this gut feeling,' Raven remarked. 'Don't ask me why. Just how sure can we be about Drake leaving the country?'

Soo made room on the table for his elbows, pushing his cup aside.

'The Ghost Squad was out at his house twenty minutes after I called Grandy. His wife told them he'd gone to Scotland on a conference. She said he'd left home about four. Grandy ordered an all-ports check and the news came through just before you people arrived. Dover says there's no question about it. Drake left on the hovercraft.'

A newspaper delivery truck roared past the café. Raven's voice was obstinate.

'If we know that Drake left the country it's because he *wants* us to know it. He's probably picked up another passport somewhere. The bastard could be on his way to Brazil by now.' The thought sickened his stomach.

Soo yawned and checked his nickel pocket watch. 'It's gone four. There's nothing we can do about it one way or another. Not tonight, in any case.' He stood up, calling his thanks to the Greek.

Raven followed him out to the street. 'You'll have to drive me home. My car's sitting in a wood sixty miles away. Which reminds me, I left Underwood's in front of the Yard.'

Soo was parked on Victoria Street. Raven let himself down in the souped-up Mini and tucked his knees up somewhere near his chin. Men were hosing the end of Buckingham Palace Road. Soo changed gear enjoying himself as he skidded the Mini across the wet tarmac.

'Cut it out!' said Raven. 'You're no James Hunt. You're making me nervous.'

Soo flicked the gearshift expertly, using two fingers. 'You're always nervous these days. You need a woman to relax you.'

'I need Drake,' answered Raven. 'How far can this Grandy be trusted, do you think?'

'As far as his ambition will take him,' said Soo. He took his eyes briefly off the road. 'Don't let that Master of Foxhounds stuff fool you. He's diamond hard under all that horseshit. Give him the chance and he'll bury Drake. He's *got* to do it out of sheer self-preservation. But like everyone else he wants to do it *his* way. Don't expect any help from him.'

He swung the Mini into a U-turn, fetching up neatly against the kerb opposite the gangway leading to Raven's houseboat. Gulls were sleeping on the television masts, their plumage rosy in the glow from the eastern sky. Raven eased himself out of the little car and poked his head back through the window.

'Thanks for the lift, Jerry. I know I'm right about Drake. I've just got to sleep on it. My love and apologies to Louise.'

Soo gave his wide square grin. 'Just remembah washing for lohndry.'

The Mini was out of sight in five seconds. Raven drew the curtains in his bedroom. He got into bed, leaving his clothes wherever they fell. He closed his eyes, carrying the niggling almost-found memory with him into a shadowy world of frantic comings and goings.

He awoke, checking the bedside clock from the nest of pillows. He was three hours later than usual but his head was clear, the enigma of the previous night resolved. He pulled back the curtains, letting in the bright daylight, drank a glass of juice and sat on the edge of the bed with the telephone on his knees. Jerry Soo was already in his office.

'Can you get me a picture of Drake?' asked Raven.

'Yes,' said Soo. 'I'll send it over in a cab. There's no time to talk now.'

A click broke the contact. Raven replaced the receiver thoughtfully. Soo's edginess was out of character, but Raven could understand. His friend had kept a low profile for two years, blending into the background and doing his thing unnoticed.

And suddenly here he was at the heart of a scandal involving the very supports of the police establishment. And he'd worry about not doing his duty. It was twenty-five past ten. Another half an hour or so and Mrs Burrows would be there. He was in no mood for bandying words with his cleaner. He hurried through his breakfast and shower, eating scrambled eggs standing up in the kitchen, wrapped in a wet towel. He dressed in his uniform of jeans, cotton shirt and sneakers and unlocked his desk. This time it was to add his old warrant card to the gun in his hip-pocket.

A couple of minutes later the doorbell rang. A taxi driver with an envelope was waiting at the end of the gangway. The picture enclosed of Drake had been cut out of a group photograph and showed him fullface, wearing his Let-Me-Be-Your-Father look. The accompanying note bore one word. *Careful!*

Raven crossed the bridge and walked through Battersea Park keeping to the paths that ran alongside the river. It was after eleven by the time he reached Vauxhall. A fleabitten ginger cat was sunning itself in the alleyway between the two paper warehouses. The Bean and Barley parking lot was empty. A waiter dressed in white fatigues tried to bar Raven's way.

'Sorry, sir. Closed. Open at twelve.'

The man's face was unfamiliar. Raven stepped around him, tapped on the door to Feldman's retreat and opened it. The fat Australian was wedged in a chair, smoking and reading the *Sporting Life*. One end of a fishing line was wrapped around a mottled fist. He looked up, taking his cigar from his teeth with his free hand.

'Shut the door, will you, mate. I don't want to set a bad example to the staff. Take a seat. And to what happy combination of circumstances do I owe the good fortune of this visit? Twice in a week is too much.'

Raven cleared the other chair of Feldman's betting-slips. 'That friend of yours who saw Drake. Who was he?'

The line jerked on Feldman's fingers. He hauled it up through the fake porthole but there was nothing on the hook. He baited it with a piece of meat from the plate of lobster scraps.

'You get a low class of fish round here. No sporting instinct. You mean Little George. I didn't think you were that much interested.'

'Never mind what you thought,' said Raven. 'I want to know just *where* he saw him.'

'Where,' repeated Feldman and coughed, dislodging an inch of ash from his cigar. 'I'm not sure. why?'

Raven took Feldman's cigar and threw it through the port-hole. He detached the fishing line from the fat man's fist and tied it to Feldman's chair.

'Now you listen to me very carefully, Sam. Who is Little George and where did he see Drake?'

Feldman's small eyes blinked cautiously. 'Now hang on a minute, Raven. I was just shooting the breeze. I don't want to be involved in anything heavy. Little George is a liar anyway.'

'No one's involving you in anything,' said Raven. 'Where and when did he see Drake?'

Feldman's fingers strayed to the fishing line, checking the tension furtively.

'A couple of months ago. Little George is out with the credit cards, you know the game. They buy what they think they can sell. I dabble for the odd box of Cubans. Apparently he saw Drake in this tobacconist shop, paying with a cheque and calling himself Bates.'

Raven's voice was patient. 'Where?'

Feldman tipped his short-necked head back and stared at the ceiling.

'Bayswater Road. He couldn't remember the name of the place but it was next to a florist.'

'How come he knows Drake if Drake doesn't know him?'

Feldman chuckled. 'Little George doesn't exactly put himself on show. Now you see now you don't. Drake wouldn't know him from a hole in the ground, but he's seen Drake. Little George was in the public gallery at the Old Bailey and Drake was giving evidence.'

Raven unlooped the fishing line and gave it back to Feldman. 'Thanks, Sam. You want to change your bait. Lobster's too rich for non-sporting fish.'

He found the tobacconist's easily enough. There was only one next to a florist's in Bayswater Road between Marble Arch and Notting Hill Gate. A sign in gilt over the doorway read:

HORACE LABERT & Successors,
Purveyors of fine tobacco

A bell tinkled as Raven pushed open the door. The furnishings were old-fashioned, the counters

mahogany with a gas cigar lighter and shelves full
of boxes of humidors. The man behind the counter
was pushing forty, but protecting the position as
best he could. His suit was silk, his thin blond hair
blow-dried and he wore a light blue eye make-up.

The eyes themselves were slightly protuberant
and snapped Raven in rapid succession as he displayed his warrant card.

'Ah yes,' he said cagily.

'Were you working here a couple of months ago?'
asked Raven.

The man bridled visibly. 'My name is Labert and
I *own* this establishment. There *is* no one else who
works here.'

Raven placed Drake's picture on the counter.
'Then you'd know this man?'

Labert lifted the flap in the counter and carried
the picture as far as the door, head on one side and
mouth pursed as he considered the likeness.

'I recognize him, yes. Why?' Labert returned the
picture and retreated to his side of the counter.

'What's his name?' demanded Raven.

Labert glanced away, fiddling with the tap of the
gas cigar lighter. A jet of flame shot in Raven's direction.

'Oops,' said Labert. 'Sorry. His name? I've no
idea.'

Raven pocketed the picture and his warrant card.
'Let's you and I understand one another thoroughly,
Mr Labert. My information is that this man bought
goods from you and paid his account by cheque.'

'With a bank card,' said Labert pertly. 'He
bought four boxes of *Partagas*. I'm running a one-

man business here as I told you, coping with V.A.T. and all the rest of it. If a customer pays by cheque. I note the number of his card and the bank guarantees the cheque up to fifty pounds. That's the end of it as far as I'm concerned. There are more things for me to do than remember names.'

'Does the name Bates mean anything to you?' Raven suggested.

Labert's blond hair shivered dissent. 'No. In any case I don't understand the purpose of your questions. You've got the man's picture in your pocket, surely you know his name.'

Raven could feel his confidence leaking. Thieves, memories were notoriously loose. Little George could well have got the name wrong or invented it to give his story the true ring of authenticity.

'Thanks for your help in any case,' he said.

Labert let him go as far as the door. 'I've an idea where he lives, though.'

Raven turned quickly. 'Where?'

Labert seemed to be enjoying his star role in a police investigation.

'I live in Sanderstead and take the train every morning to Victoria. Then I walk across the Park, rain or shine. It must have been about a week after your friend had bought the cigars that I saw him coming out of that big block at Albion Gate. I can tell you the time if that's important. Five to nine. That's the time that I cross the road there.'

Plymouth Towers turned out to be a complex of three ten-storey blocks built in the shape of an H. The ends of the vertical wings faced the Park and gardens. Fountains and fish ponds extended on each flank of the lateral bar. Raven walked around the block, checking it out from the pavement. The main entrance was on a side street and staffed by four uniformed porters. The cars parked in front were expensive, many of them sporting C.D. plates. Raven counted eight alternative ways to enter or leave the complex, all of the doors unattended. Against that, the corridors could well be centrally controlled by television.

He crossed Bayswater Road and sat on a bench near the grass staring over at the elegant architecture. It didn't matter what other people thought, instinct told him that Drake was somewhere in there sitting snugly while the hunt took off in all directions. The man had the cunning of an old bull water buffalo and was equally dangerous. Whoever he was at the moment, whatever guise he'd assumed, the identity would have been well-established. An *alter ego* to don like a magician's cloak and disappear whenever danger pressed. Drake must have been living under the threat of disclosure for years, like the rest of the gang who were on the take. The web that stretched from the Yard was hypersensitive. The impact of a foreign body would set up the kind of vibrations that would warn Drake to be off and running. His recognition by a small-time thief two months previously was a chance in a million. The odds were heavily against Drake giving anything else away.

It was getting on for half past twelve by his watch. It was tempting to toy with the idea of walking into the main entrance of Plymouth Court and pulling the same stunt he had used on the tobacconist. But porters in expensive apartment buildings tended to be protective of their tenants. Not only that, the faintest scent of danger would dissipate Drake into thin air. If he *was* really there. A few more knots tied themselves in Raven's stomach. He *had* to be there and there must be a way of establishing it. He walked south keeping to the grass till he reached the bridge that crossed the Serpentine. It seemed a long time since he had rediscovered Campbell. A taxi dropped him on the Embankment. Mrs Burrows had been and gone, leaving the sitting room sweet with the smell of freesias. Going through to the kitchen, he lifted the cover of the still-warm casserole. A note left on the kitchen table identified the contents.

This is Galician Tuna Salad. You owe me one pound for the flowers. Leave todays money with tomorrows. Nelly Burrows.

A warm tuna salad defeated him but he spooned some of it onto a plate and took it through to the sitting room. The cold *Budweiser* helped it down. He put Fritz Kreisler's *Caprice Viennoise* on the player and lowered the arm. He sat in the sunshine, eyes closed luxuriating in the music's sudden changes of mood. When the record stopped, he picked up the telephone, still hearing the sad strains of the violin. He called the Yard and asked for Jerry Soo.

'Thanks for the picture. Are you able to talk?'

'Not for too long.'

Raven paced with the phone to the end of the extension line. 'Have you heard anything yet?'

'Not a lot, no. Nobody's talking at this end. The word is that Grandy's taken off for somewhere, but his secretary doesn't know where. The Ghost Squad cleared Drake's office and Underwood is in a cell in Cannon Row police station. They're supposed to be charging him sometime today. And nobody knows the trouble I've seen.'

'I think I know where Drake is,' said Raven. He lowered his voice and explained how and where.

Soo sounded doubtful. 'There was a report in an hour or so ago that he'd been sighted in Brussels. A fellow in the Interpol office told me.'

'Wishful thinking,' said Raven.

'Have it your own way,' his friend replied. 'I suppose we could organize a door-to-door. We'd need to get hold of Grandy first for an authorization.'

Raven bent into the telephone. 'Fuck Grandy! The last thing we want is a door-to-door search. Drake would smell it a mile away. There are over four hundred apartments in that complex. I've got another idea.'

'Good,' said Soo. His voice changed suddenly, assuming the tone of authority. 'You'll have to put your inquiry in writing, sir, and address it to the Home Office.'

Raven was no sooner out on deck than the telephone rang. It was Arbela Stewart on the line from Heathrow Airport.

'We've been trying to reach you all morning. It's all set. We're flying out in half an hour's time.'

'Terrific,' said Raven. The one o'clock factory whistle blew in Battersea Power Station and the Great Dane on the neighbouring houseboat started to howl. Raven closed the door leading out to the deck. 'Don't forget there's a law against taking sterling out of the country. No more than fifty pounds.'

'I banked it this morning,' she announced. 'The manager's taking care of the transfer. Aren't you even going to ask where we're going?'

'No,' said Raven. 'Just as long as you are going.'

'You're a strange man,' she said. Her voice was warm. 'But I think I love you. Hang on a minute, here's Roderic. We're getting married as soon as we land.'

Campbell was oddly at a loss. 'Well, this is it and thanks for everything. I threw the gun away, incidentally.'

'Good,' said Raven. 'And congratulations.' A thought suddenly hit him. 'Plymouth Towers, Albion Gate. Do you know it?'

'Sure I know it,' said Campbell. 'The Burglar's Grave. Look, that's a very strange thing to ask under the circumstances.'

'You mean those side entrances aren't as innocent as they look?'

He could hear the flight announcements in the background. Campbell's answer was hurried.

'What the hell are you up to, Raven?'

'Finishing what you promised to help me do. Can I get into that building without being seen?'

Campbell's voice changed. 'I'm doing what you

told me to do. If you want me to cancel the flight and help, O.K.'

'Answering the question's enough,' said Raven. 'Yes or no?'

'Yes,' said Campbell. 'The second door going north after the main entrance. You take the stone steps just inside down to the central-heating plant. Wintertime there's always an engineer on duty. I don't know about summer. They used to spend their time drinking tea and watching television. You'll see their room. If you get past that there's a door at the far end. It's fire- and water-proof. That'll lead you out to the service elevators. And look out for closed-circuit TV cameras. *Bonne chance* as we sophisticates say.'

'So long,' said Raven. 'And take care of that girl.' A few more minutes would close one chapter, but the end of the story was still to be written.

He stripped down to his shorts, put the bolt on the gangway door and sprawled out on the river side of the deck. Hot sunshine released the scent of the stocks and the lemon-verbena. The Great Dane on the next boat had stopped howling and had gone back to sleep. There was no one nearer than the opposite bank to oversee him. He turned on his back, trying to remember what they had taught at the Hari Krishna Meditation Centre. *Concentrate on the Middle Eye and Rid The Body of Weight.* A couple of minutes proved enough. He was unable to locate his Middle Eye and felt every ounce of his hundred and eighty pounds. All of which figured, he thought, since he'd finally had to bust the Guru and the Guru's lady for False Pretences and running a brothel.

He pulled himself up on a chair and put his feet in a box of sand that he kept for cleaning fouled decks. The coarse grains ran pleasantly between his toes. People were on his mind. Campbell, the girl, Jerry and Louise, his sister. And most of all, Drake. If he could see himself as they did, maybe it would help and reason told him that he was going to need all the help he could get. Take Jerry Soo, for instance. Jerry saw him as the loner, the deliberate breaker of rules. For his sister he was a man who lacked a sense of responsibility. Each of them was possibly right in some degree but the basic truth about him, the one that provided his motor, remained undiscovered. And yet it was simple. He could forgive the failures of others but never his own.

He threw the remainder of Mrs Burrows' exotic tuna salad over the side and dressed again. He was doubtful about taking the gun with him this time, but he finally put it in his pocket along with the unauthorized warrant card. If you're on your way to rob a bank you don't worry about parking tickets.

It was three o'clock. He called the Royal Automobile Club and arranged to have his car collected from the country. There was a spare set of ignition-keys in a magnetized holder under the rear bumper. He locked up the houseboat and walked north as far as King's Road Public Library. The people using the Reference Room didn't seem to have moved since the last time he had been there, down to the snoring old man with the broken-veined face.

An assistant gave Raven a red box containing the Electors Lists for the City of Westminster. He carried them to a reading table. Sun slanted through the dusty atmosphere, striking the polished surface. The lists marked A were the ones currently in force and had been compiled the previous February. With any sort of luck Drake would figure on them somewhere. A recent law required every householder or tenant of furnished and unfurnished premises to declare the names and ages of all people living under his roof. Raven found the list for Albion Gate classified as being in the Hyde Park Ward in the Parliamentary Constituency of Westminster, Paddington. The entries for Plymouth Towers took up six pages. He thumbed through them rapidly without finding a Bates. The nearest was Batch, John Michael. But there was no guarantee that Drake wouldn't have ignored his legal requirement, no clue to the name he might be using as occupant of the flat. The one certainty was that he'd be living alone. It was an act of faith now for Raven that Drake was in there somewhere. He copied the names and flat numbers of all the male, single tenants. There were seventeen, located on six floors in the three blocks of the building.

He returned the box of voters' lists and started walking north again, the sunshine on his back, his thoughts for the moment with Arbela and Campbell. There'd be comebacks if it were known what he had done with the North Koreans' twenty thousand pounds. People wouldn't be at a loss for an adjective to describe his behaviour. Quixotic, irresponsible, even downright criminal. Yet the alternative would have been confiscation. As it was, the cash was a kind of springboard for the Canadian couple and they had as much chance of landing safely as anyone.

He bought a felt pen and reporters' pad and began to plan his moves. Drake must have gone to ground as soon as he'd doubled back from France. He could well be ready to stay there holed-up for months if necessary. On the other hand he might be heavily disguised, his exits and entrances part of his new identity. The best time to hit Plymouth Towers was between six and seven. People would have returned from business and were not likely to have gone out again. He joined the first rush of late-afternoon passengers on the Underground. They were school children for the most part on their way home from the Queen's Gate academies. He left the train at Bayswater and strolled south into the cosmopolitan shopping area. He made his purchases in a sporting-goods store and carried them into the Park. The instructions on the four canisters were written in five languages. He rewrapped them in the plastic bag, making a tight bundle that he could carry more easily.

Beyond the Park railings, Plymouth Towers soared above the constant stream of traffic, secure and affluent-looking. The gardens were green in the spray blowing from the fountains, the canopies over the entrances with candy-striped canvas. He raised his head, casting his glance down the rows of windows. It wouldn't be long now nor could it have ended in any other way. Just Drake and him, locked in the final battle. At six o'clock he threw away his cigarette and crossed Bayswater Road again, the wrapped canisters under his arm. He walked past the main entrance to Plymouth Towers, looking straight ahead. As he reached the third doorway he stepped sideways smartly. A no man's land of thickly carpeted corridor led to more glass doors. Beyond them were the first floor flats. He could see the closed-circuit television Campbell had warned him about, the two scanning lens fixed high on the wall. A flight of concrete steps on his left led down to the basement areas. His sneakers made no sound as he made his way down. He opened an inch of the heavy door on to a vista of oil-burning furnaces and air-conditioning units. Giant hooded extractors vanished through the ceilings. Steel and copper glowed under hundred-watt lamps. A loud humming noise made a barrier between the ear and all other sound. Raven pushed the door open another inch. The lighted control-room was twenty yards away, close enough for him to see the dials on the panels, the man with the greasy cap sitting with his back to Raven. Raven wasted no time, slipping through the door and backing off towards the machines, keeping his eyes all the time on the control-room. Ten seconds took him to the far side of the subterranean room, putting a bank of machinery between him and the engineer. It was ten degrees hotter than up on the street and he was starting to sweat.

The door Campbell had spoken about was at the other end, an asbestos-lined affair of heavy steel that was proofed against fire and water. A two-position handle allowed it to be loosely locked or completely sealed. He lifted the handle and the bulky door opened under his pressure. He slipped through the narrow space and pulled the lever on the other side. He was standing in a well at the bottom of the service lift shaft. He brought the cage down, a bare boxlike structure with an iron-slatted wooden floor. In the cage were three twenty-gallon drums of primer paint. He took the lift up to the seventh floor and stepped out on to the service-stairway. The television cameras were only installed at street level. There was no control on the upper floors. The first name on his list for Plymouth Towers West was *Marcus Evander, flat W702*.

The corridor was quieter and cooler with niches where reproduction side tables were set with vases of red carnations. He took out his pen and pad and rang the doorbell. There was movement inside and the door opened on a length of chain. A record was playing flute music and there was a glimpse of mobiles hanging in the hallway. The man looking out was wearing red slippers and robe and a spliced wig that had loosened with the growth of his hair.

'Yes?'

'Mr Evander?' Raven put a tick against the name. 'Good evening, sir. I'm from the *Friends of the Forest Society*. We're a voluntary non-profit organization concerned with the preservation of tradi-tional values. I wonder if you'd mind answering a few questions?'

Evander's voice was tart. 'Whose traditional values are we talking about?'

Raven blinked. All he wanted to do was check

the apartments and get out of there as quickly as possible without leaving any suspicion behind.

'Those of the Western World,' said Raven.

'They stink,' Evander said in a very clear voice and slammed the door shut.

Bridging passages connected the three wings at each level. There was no one else on Raven's list living on either of the seventh floors. He started working his way down. By five to seven he'd rung fourteen doorbells. All but two of the tenants had been at home, answering Raven's banal inquiries with tolerance, incredulity and in one case moral indignation. He was now on the fourth floor in Plymouth Towers East, *E420, Paul Hagan*. It was the last flat in the corridor, fifty yards from the nearest lift but close to the service staircase at the end of the wing. There was no doorbell, nothing but a small brass knocker cast in the shape of a laurel wreath. The noise it made echoed sharply, less the sound of brass than of steel. It left him with an odd feeling of uncertainty and he let the knocker fall again. The sound chased itself along the corridor. There was nothing from inside. His mind and body seemed to swell and he felt that this could be it, that it was Drake on the other side of this door.

Raven stepped away quickly from the inspection glass, along the carpet and through the swing doors on to the concrete stairway. He knelt on the third step down, looking under the swing doors along the corridor. His senses had sharpened. He could hear the traffic along Bayeswater Road, smell the passage of countless dogs over the rough concrete surface near his face. But the only thing that mattered was what he saw. It was a couple of minutes before the door of E420 was opened. A slit at first then inches. And the eyes there became a face, Drake's beefy face, cautious as he glanced both ways along the corridor. Then the door was closed again.

Raven lifted himself up and dusted off his jeans. He was sweating profusely and his mouth was parched. He was certain that Drake hadn't seen him. Cupboards on the service-staircase landings housed a collection of mops and pails. He hid his canisters in one of them and made his way down to the street level. He left Plymouth Towers by the main entrance. The porters supervising the busy lobby were dealing with baggage, a car-hire driver and a delivery of flowers. The one nearest the street spun the revolving doors for Raven, touching the peak of his cap. Raven walked south, away from Drake's windows, forcing himself into a casual stroll in the cool of the evening. He was suddenly calm, outwardly calm and inwardly excited. He was like a man in the woods with a rook-rifle, his quarry in the sights, his finger on the trigger. It was desperately important not to pull the trigger too soon. He was only getting one shot.

He called Jerry Soo's number from a call-box in Bayswater Station.

'I've got him, Jerry! I was right and I've got him!' He was unable to keep the excitement out of his voice. Nothing else seemed to matter. Nothing else *did* matter. 'Did you hear what I said, Jerry?'

'I heard,' Soo answered. 'Grandy's back by the way. If he ever went.'

Grandy's return increased the chance of prompt

and efficient action. The trick would be in controlling it. At the back of Raven's mind was the constant fear that even now Drake might escape. He had to be flushed out into the open, his earth stopped and then hunted down.

'I want you to call Grandy personally,' Raven said earnestly. 'Don't take no for an answer. Give him the place and the time, but insist that it's done my way. We'll need plainclothesmen covering all the entrances to Plymouth Towers. Experienced men who know what they're doing. No cowboys. Get them there at twenty hours precisely, Jerry. That's eight o'clock. Twenty hours. O.K.?'

'Got it,' said Soo. 'Have you actually seen him?'

Soo's voice might have sounded offhand to anyone else but Raven knew better.

'I've seen the bastard, Jerry.'

'And couldn't he have seen you?'

'No.' Raven wiped his neck. He was sure of what he said. 'Otherwise he'd have made his break right away.' People in apartment buildings often knocked on the wrong door and moved away without making explanations. No, Drake would be sitting up there quite happily.

'How do you figure on getting him out?'

'It's all under control,' said Raven. 'Just you do what I ask and, Jerry – be there yourself!'

He entered Plymouth Towers the way he had left, walking to the lifts unchallenged. He skulked on the top floor of the West Wing, watching the street below. At eight o'clock exactly a couple of unmarked V8 Rovers pulled out of Bayswater Road. Each dropped its crew of four. Eight men, casually dressed, who drifted apart to stand in the shade of the trees or stroll in the gardens. It was all Raven needed to see. The rest of the building would be covered. He ran down the service stairway in the East Wing and retrieved his canisters. He shouldered through the swing doors on the third floor and walked as far as the nearest flower display. Pulling the rings on two of the canisters, he stood them upright on the floor under the table. Black smoke billowed along the corridor. He ran for the stairs, punched the fire alarm as he went. Bells jangled in all directions, mingling with the blare of what sounded like a foghorn. He skidded across the concrete and rammed the last canisters under the table twenty feet from Drake's apartment. More smoke belched out. He could hear doors slamming, people shouting. He backed through the swing doors and waited.

GEORGE DRAKE

July 21

He moved away from the open sitting room window. He had spent most of the day there in an armchair, the net curtains in front of him blowing in the faint breeze. Already he'd established patterns in the scene below. The gradual filling of the Park with dogs, children and picnickers, the jockey-capped riders who trotted their mounts along the bridle paths.

Life wasn't going to be easy, cooped-up for the rest of the summer, through autumn and on into winter. It would be six months' confinement to the day. It was good to be precise about things like that. Six calendar months took him to January 20. The hunt for him would have slackened by then, the urgency gone from it. His picture and his description would have been replaced by those of others. He could see it all now, the last look around the flat before he turned out the lights. One small bag would be enough for his needs, something big enough to hold a change of underwear, his money, documents and cigars. He'd leave the building by one of the side exits. The street lamps would be burning, people muffled against the wind. The booking was already made.

A Week in the United Kingdom, French-style! One Glorious Week in a Jersey Four Star Hotel for only £120! Return Flight, Three Meals a Day, Service Charges and V.A.T. Included!

Jersey was thirty-seven nautical miles from St

179

Malo and Brittany, with a winter ferry service once a day. He could leave at nine in the morning. By the time his absence was noticed he'd be a couple of thousand miles away with yet another identity.

He settled down again in his chair with his guide-books. He'd worked out half a dozen ways from France to Brazil. His favourite was by train from St Malo to Lisbon and by Varig Airlines to Rio de Janeiro. He already had his visa. Regulations required a certificate of good character supplied by the police. It had given him a lot of pleasure to prepare his own, beautifully typed on official Scotland Yard stationery.

To Whom It May Concern

This is to certify that Humphrey Bates, New Zealand citizen and holder of New Zealand passport No: C 297648 is a person of probity, good faith and high moral standing.

Signed   *George Drake, Commander*

'Probity, good faith and high moral standing'. It had a good ring and he had found it on a gravestone near Rye.

Brazil, he read, *the most extensive state of South America, unequalled for its rivers. Varig of Brazil and eight foreign airlines operate services between Brazil and Europe. More than five million passengers passed through Brazilian airports in 1976, Rio de Janeiro and Sao Paulo alone accounting for two million arrivals and departures.*

He liked that, visualizing constant streams of

tropical-clothed people in gaily-banded straw hats, all of high moral standing and probity, welcomed by customs and police alike.

He closed his eyes again, switching to a wide beach lined with coconut palms. Spray blew in his face across the empty sand and he smelled the exotic flowers. Vila Lobo, a fishing village tucked in behind the headland, an hour's drive from Salvador. The priest's house had stood empty for seventeen years, the lemons and oranges rotting on the surrounding ground. He'd paid less than four thousand pounds for the place. Fresh fish, cheap cigars and an endless supply of nubile girls who would keep him young. He'd do the same as the other escapers did, the Great Train Robbers and fugitive financiers, the ex-Nazis. Make a new world for himself and settle down to his book. *The Story of My Life* by Commander Drake of the Yard. Dedicated to all those assholes who made it possible.

It was almost six o'clock and time for the news. He put his books on the floor and switched on the radio. His flat was the last in the corridor with the outside wall of his bathroom facing the service stairway and lift. The residents' lifts were twenty-five yards away. He only had one set of neighbours to worry about. The only proof of their existence was the occasional sound of voices as they came or went. He'd never set eyes on either the man or the woman. But he was ultra-careful, using a doctor's stethoscope to determine when his neighbours were in or out, flushing his lavatory cistern only in their absence. He had no telephone and the brass on his front door stayed tarnished. Most of the time he watched his portable TV with the sound off. He'd put his rowing machine in the bathroom. This was the way he was going to keep fit. A gentle row for half an hour every morning, resting whenever he grew tired and the occasional stroll along the corridor when the rest of the block was asleep. He needed no more exercise. He was as fit if not fitter than most people of his age and the medicine cabinet was stocked with standard remedies

The news gave the latest information about the Arab-Jewish conflict, a situation that left him indifferent. Both were equally objectionable as far as he was concerned, poxy pests who should be left to deal with each other. The news bulletin made no reference either to him, Underwood or the North Koreans. The omission neither surprised nor deceived him. He'd had his warning and acted on it, without waiting for details. It was enough to know that the Koreans were in trouble. His well-laid plans for survival were a constant source of pleasure to him, like the Chinese boxes he remembered seeing somewhere, one fitting inside the other, the secret contained in the last. And the secret was his.

He was out in the kitchen, making himself a sandwich to go with his tea when he heard the knock at his front door. He put the breadknife down very slowly, turning his head towards the hall. Whoever was outside knocked again, the noise ringing in Drake's ears like a blacksmith's hammer on the anvil. He wet his lips furtively, feeling the sweat starting to drip under his light cashmere robe. He moved almost gracefully for a man of his build, tip-toeing to the front door. The bubble-glass inspection hole gave him a forty five-degree glimpse in both directions. He could see no one. He went back into the kitchen. The breadknife was still in his hand, but he had lost his appetite. His tea was already poured. He raised the cup and drank thirstily. It was obviously someone who had made a mistake, a porter perhaps, trying to deliver goods to the wrong apartment.

He tiptoed into the hall again and opened his front door, an inch at first and then wider. There was nobody in sight.

All hell broke loose over an hour later. Alarm bells were ringing everywhere, one of them vibrating on his outside wall. The foghorns were booming in all directions. He smelled the smoke seconds later. Voices were shouting nearby and a woman screamed He acted quickly, slipping into trousers, shirt and jacket. He stuffed his New Zealand passport in his pocket along with his other documents and stepped out of his flat into a smoke-filled corridor. The screaming woman was close to him now. He pushed past her halfseen figure and turned sharp left, avoiding the rush for the residents' lifts. Smoke was everywhere, but he could distinguish the strips of sunshine at the bottom of the doors leading to the service staircase. The Fire Brigade would be on its way by now. In the meantime it was important to retain his anonymity and get back to the flat just as soon as the blaze was under control. Had the knock on his door come from someone trying to alert him to danger, someone who had smelled the smoke earlier and run blindly, banging on the nearest doors?

He put his handkerchief in his pocket and stepped forward, pushing the swing doors that led to the concrete stairway.

JOHN RAVEN & GEORGE DRAKE

July 21

He was just inside the swing-doors, the gun in his hand. He'd brought the service lift up to the fourth floor and the cage was open, holding it there. Smoke was filtering into the well of the staircase from both floors and it was no longer possible to see through the windows, but he could hear fire engines barrelling along Bayswater Road. His body tightened. He remembered the instructions printed on the canisters.

Distress signals for campers, sailors, sportsmen etc. emitting a dense fog of chemical smoke guaranteed to function for up to one hour in all known climatic conditions.

Up to one hour. It would take time for them to find the source of the alarm and in the meantime panic ruled on the third and fourth floors. Men were shouting. A woman screamed against a background of jangling bells and the blare of the foghorn.

The doors swung open suddenly under the pressure of Drake's shoulder, allowing more smoke to billow into the stairwell. Raven's eyes were beginning to redden and smart but he froze for a second, the two men registering recognition and hatred. They moved simultaneously, Drake's heavy arm lifting in a clubbing motion, Raven jamming his gun in the other man's belly. He took the weight of Drake's blow on the side of the head, barely feeling it.

'Move!' he said hoarsely. His gaze locked on Drake's as the older man backed into the lift. Raven slammed the gate and pressed the first-floor button. Drake's cheeks had drained of colour, leaving his flesh with the appearance of suet. His shirt was on inside out and blobs of spittle lodged in the corners of his mouth.

The cage descended slowly, a clank announcing the passing of each floor. There was no shake in Raven's gun-hand. His excitement had left him completely. He felt that he was doing something he had done in the past, over and over again, waking and sleeping. And that this was the last time he'd do it.

He smiled without knowing it, hiding his tired-ness and relief. 'One thing, whenever you go to your cell at night, remember who put you there.'

The blood was returning to Drake's face redden-ing his ears and his jowls. His eyes were like those of a cornered animal. Losing, he defied defeat. He opened his mouth as if to reply, but said nothing. The cage stopped. Raven yanked the gate, nodding at the pass door on their left.

'Through that door!'

It let them into the main lobby crowded with tenants clutching children, pets and possessions. There were firemen and porters clustered close to the revolving doors. In front of them was Colonel Grandy flanked by a group of plainclothesmen. Jerry Soo was standing nearby, his eyes fixed on Raven and Drake. The babble subsided as the two men crossed the hall then a woman shrieked.

'Look out! He's got a gun!'

People moved away hurriedly, making a path for them. Grandy came forward, surrounded by faces from Raven's past. The Commissioner's mouth was tight, an avenging angel in pinstriped blue flannel. He looked long into Drake's eyes then signalled to one of the detectives.

'Take him away,' he said contemptuously.

Raven watched the small group, Drake in the middle, till it reached the police car waiting outside. He was conscious of the sudden quiet. All the fire alarms had been silenced. Grandy was watching him, eyebrows quizzical. He managed to make an insult of his question.

'I suppose those cameramen and reporters outside are for you?'

Raven took a deep breath, then pulled the gun and warrant card from his pocket and handed them to Grandy.

'You can do what you like with these, Colonel. And there's something I want to tell you before we part. You're one of the most insufferable pricks I've ever met. Goodnight.'

Soo followed him through the revolving doors, kicking at the flagged pathway with the toes of his basketball boots.

'There's something I have to tell *you*, John.'

Raven heard through a wall of anger. 'Is it good or bad?'

'It's whatever you make of it,' answered Soo. 'I

put this whole thing on paper two days ago. I *had* to, John. I'm still a cop.'

Raven said nothing, but his brain was busy. 'Two pages of it,' Soo went on. 'But without mentioning Campbell incidentally. I did what I thought was right.'

Raven nodded. 'Good for you. So?'

Soo grinned. 'The report's still with the head-hunters. Venables made it plain that he didn't believe me.'

'He believed you all right,' said Raven. 'And so did the guy who tipped off Drake. Ah well, that's what you get for doing your duty, my friend. You're in the wrong line of business.'

Soo's grin widened. 'I can think of worse. By the way, this last performance of yours is going to be a hard one to follow.'

'I know,' said Raven.

The small man quickened step to match Raven's stride. 'Aren't you ever going to learn to leave well alone, for crissakes?'

Newsreel cameramen were filming the two of them as they made their way through the garden. The reporters were ready with their microphones.

'No,' said Raven, 'I don't think I am.' And this time his smile came easily.

〉〉〉 If you've enjoyed this book and would like to discover more great vintage crime and thriller titles, as well as the most exciting crime and thriller authors writing today, visit: 〉〉〉

The Murder Room
Where Criminal Minds Meet

themurderroom.com